THE PATTER OF TINY FEET AT THE STABLES ON MUDDYPUDDLE LANE

Heart-warming, uplifting romance

Etti Summers

Copyright © 2023 Etti Summers
Published by Lilac Tree Books

This book is licensed for your personal enjoyment only. This book may not be re-sold or given away to other people. If you would like to share this book with another person, please purchase an additional copy for each recipient. If you're reading this book and did not purchase it, or it was not purchased for your use only, then please purchase your own copy. Thank you for respecting the hard work of this author.

This story is a work of fiction. All names, characters, places and incidents are invented by the author or have been used fictitiously and are not to be construed as real. Any similarity to actual persons or events is purely coincidental.

The author asserts the moral rights under the Copyright, Design and Patents Act 1988 to be identified as the author of this work.

All rights reserved. No part of this publication may be reproduced, stored in a retrieval system or transmitted, in any form or by any means without the prior consent of the author, nor be otherwise circulated in any form of binding or cover other than that which it is published and without a similar condition being imposed on the subsequent purchaser.

CHAPTER ONE

Isaac Richards pulled into the car park of the stables on Muddypuddle Lane, grabbed his document case from the back seat, then clambered out and glanced around. The yard was as immaculate as always, with hardly a blade of straw out of place. Despite being about seven months pregnant, Petra ran a tight ship.

It was a short walk across the yard to the farmhouse and as he made his way towards it, he passed several loose boxes with their doors open. A couple of others had an equine head poking over the top, the owner's ears twitching as the animals followed his progress. He could hear music and voices coming from one of the stables and he wondered whether he should let whoever-it-was know he was here, or whether he should carry on up to the house and knock on the door.

The decision was taken out of his hands when a woman reversed out of the stable, dragging a loaded wheelbarrow. As she glanced over her shoulder to see where she was going, she spotted him.

'Petra, your architect is here,' she called, manoeuvring the barrow so that it rested next to the wall.

Out of habit and even though he'd met October on his previous visits to the stables, Isaac held out his hand. October wiped hers on her backside, began to reach out to shake his, then hesitated.

'I don't think it's a good idea,' she said, and she showed him her palm. It was daubed with green-coloured muck and Isaac was fairly certain he knew what it was.

He settled for saying, 'Hi,' and smiling at her.

'Isaac!' Petra emerged from the stable. 'Shall we go into the house? Amos, Harry and Nathan are already there. We're just waiting for the builder to arrive.'

Isaac chuckled. 'I've yet to meet a builder who's on time.' This would be the first time he'd meet the builder Petra and Harry had decided to use, and he was interested to see who they'd plumped for, considering he'd be working fairly closely with the guy.

Petra frowned. 'Actually, it isn't the builder who is late – you're early,' she pointed out.

'You know I hate being late,' he said, following her around the side of the house and into a boot room.

Petra toed off her Wellington boots and shoved her feet into a pair of pumps. He caught a glimpse of horses woven into the fabric of her socks and smiled.

'What?' she demanded, noticing the direction of his gaze. 'Doesn't everyone have horsey socks?'

Isaac thought of his own plain black socks and wished he was wearing more inspiring ones as he began to remove his shoes.

'No need to take them off,' Petra told him, 'Just as long as they aren't covered in mud.'

They weren't, although they were rather scuffed and scruffy, and hinted more towards the steel toe-cap end of the footwear market than the loafer side. He also kept a pair of sturdy work boots in his car for when he was on site, as building work tended to be a mucky business.

Petra led him through a higgledy-piggledy kitchen redolent with the aroma of coffee and baking bread, and into a dining room where three men were already seated.

'Amos, Harry, Nathan...' Isaac nodded to them and sat down. He'd met Amos who owned the stables, and Harry, who was Petra's fiancé, several times over the course of the past few months, but he'd only met Nathan, the stables' general manager, once or twice before.

As he opened his document case, slid out a rolled-up bundle and spread the drawings out, Isaac wondered which of them was going to manage the build.

'Congratulations on obtaining planning permission,' he began. 'I expect you're relieved it didn't take very long. The process can sometimes trundle on for months, so you're lucky.'

'Luck has got nothing to do with it,' a woman's voice said from behind. 'It's because they've got a good architect.'

Isaac stiffened. Straightening slowly, he turned around, wanting desperately to believe he was mistaken, but at the same time praying that he wasn't.

'Hello, Isaac, long time no see,' the woman added.

'**Nelly**.' His reply was barely louder than a whisper and he cleared his throat, conscious of everyone's eyes on him. 'How are you?'

'Do you two know each other?' Petra asked.

'We go way back,' Nelly replied. Her gaze bored into him, pinning him like a moth to a board.

'It's good to see you,' Isaac said, hastily trying to compose himself.

'You, too.'

Harry half-rose. 'Nelly, take a seat. I was about to make more coffee before we start. Can I get you anything?'

'A coffee would be great,' she said, sitting down.

'Isaac?' Harry turned his attention to him.

'Er, no thanks.' Isaac couldn't drag his gaze away from Nelly. '**You're** the builder!' he blurted.

'I am. Have you got a problem with that?' Her voice was as sultry as he remembered, velvet over steel. She was as forthright as he remembered, too. He could almost see her bristling.

'No problem,' he assured her, but he was lying. He most definitely **did** have a problem. But it had nothing to do with her being a female builder in a predominantly male profession. It was because of Nelly, herself. 'How is your dad?' he asked.

'He died a while back.'

Isaac saw the pain in her eyes. 'I'm sorry to hear that. I know how close you were.'

Harry returned to the dining room and placed a tray containing several mugs of steaming black coffee on the table, along with a jug of milk and a bowl of sugar. Despite Isaac saying he didn't want a drink, Harry had made him one anyway.

Nelly added milk to hers, then picked it up and took a sip, and Isaac's gaze was drawn to her mouth. How many times had he kissed those lips? Would they taste the same, feel the same?

As though she could tell what he was thinking, Nelly caught his eye and he blushed, hastily looking away.

Nelly said. 'Can I take a look?' She gestured to the plans.

'Be my guest.'

While she studied the drawings, Isaac studied her.

The changes the years had made to her were subtle. Shorter hair, but not by very much. More angular cheekbones, the youthful roundness she'd had when she was a student having morphed into a more mature beauty. Eyes more guarded, expression less open. But essentially she was still the same Nelly that he had loved and lost.

'No amendments?' she asked after a few moments.

Isaac was abruptly dragged back to the matter at hand, and he realised she was referring to the plans. She would have seen the basic set of drawings when she was quoting for the contract, but not these most recent ones.

'Only a small one – here.' He pointed to the addition of a window high up on the gable end. 'Fire regs,' he explained.

Nora nodded. 'That's fine.'

'Will that affect the quote?' Petra asked, her gaze on Nelly.

Nelly was drinking tea, not the coffee she'd favoured when he had known her, Isaac noticed. Wasn't it odd what the mind focused on when it had been blind-sided? He should have expected to bump into her at some point though, now that he was back on her turf, and he felt foolish not to have braced himself for it.

'Yes, but only by a marginal amount,' Nelly assured Petra, and Isaac snapped

back into focus as he reminded himself
that this wasn't a trip down memory lane
– he had a job to do.

'I'll be honest with you,' Petra said to her.
'We need to keep the costs down. How
much preparatory work can we effectively
do ourselves before you need to step in?'

Nelly shrugged. 'You can do quite a bit,
up to, but not including knocking walls
down, unless you're confident about
supporting the roof adequately. The shed
needs to be emptied, obviously, the
partitions need removing, the floor needs
to be dug down half a metre. It depends
on how soon you want me to start and
how long it will take you to get it build-
ready.'

Isaac tuned out as Harry and Nathan
discussed the feasibility of doing the
preparatory work themselves, with Amos

and Petra chipping in with the occasional comment. Nelly, he noticed, was mostly silent. Outwardly she seemed to be focusing on her clients, but he had a feeling she was as aware of him as he was of her.

From the second he'd heard her voice he'd tingled from his head to his toes and his pulse had raced.

Sipping the coffee he hadn't thought he'd wanted, and now grateful for anything to help with the dryness in his mouth, he kept glancing at her over the rim of his mug. And each time he did so, her eyes flickered as though she'd been watching him, and had looked away before he'd caught her.

He wasn't sure how he felt about Nelly Newsome coming back into his life, but he did know one thing – he didn't intend to let her into his heart for a second time.

Not when she'd broken it once before.

Isaac kept glancing at her. Nelly could feel his gaze on her face, as real as a finger stroking her cheek.

He used to do that, she recalled suddenly...trace a finger down her face from the corner of her eye to her mouth; then he would run that same finger across her lips until she couldn't stand the delicious tickle of it. She'd catch it in her mouth, and her nibbling on his finger always led to—

Enough, she told herself. It was in the past and that's where it should stay. There was no point remembering what they had once meant to each other, and she certainly shouldn't be thinking about it right now. She needed to focus on her clients and the job at hand, not on how deeply she had once been in love with Isaac Richards. Anyway, it was a long time ago. They had both moved on with their lives. It was just unfortunate that they now had to work together. It was also unfortunate that Petra hadn't mentioned her architect by name when she'd spoken to Nelly, so that Nelly could have prepared herself. But at least Isaac had looked as shocked as Nelly had felt when he'd seen her, so Petra hadn't mentioned her name to him either. It was a small consolation.

All she hoped was that no one had noticed her reaction to him. At least she'd had a tiny bit of warning when she'd seen him sitting at the table, and although he'd had his back to her she would have recognised him anywhere, even if he hadn't spoken. It was just enough warning to stamp down on the sudden lurch her heart had given. Thank goodness October had shown her into the house and had disappeared before Nelly had heard that so-familiar voice, because she'd slapped a hand to her chest and her knees had almost failed her. She'd had to take a deep breath to steady herself, and only then had she been able to walk into the room with a professional smile on her face and a quip on her lips.

Damn and blast, but he was still as attractive as ever. More so, if she was honest. He'd always been a handsome devil with his tall, rangy frame and broad shoulders, and that face – it had been to die for. He'd worn his hair longer then, probably because he preferred to spend his money in the pub rather than in the barbershop, and he'd had permanent stubble on his face because his razor was constantly blunt. She had rather liked the look, despite the rash she'd had on her cheek from it. His chin was smooth now and she wondered if his skin would feel as soft as it looked.

That was the only soft thing about him she saw, as she studied him out of the corner of her eye. His stomach appeared to be washboard hard underneath the white shirt he wore, and she could just see the tops of his thighs and how the material of his trousers stretched across the underlying muscles.

Oh, poo, he'd caught her looking, and she hastily dropped her eyes to the table and the plans lying on it.

There was another part of him that was soft for the briefest of moments, and that was the expression in his eyes. But when she risked shooting him another swift look (she didn't seem able to help herself – he drew her gaze like iron filings to a magnet) his expression was blank, and his eyes were hooded.

Her heart thudded uncomfortably as she realised that he'd worn the exact same guarded expression the last time she'd set eyes on him. He'd been distant and wary, with no hint of the pain she knew she'd caused him.

But what else was she supposed to have done? She'd been between a rock and a hard place, and she'd loved him too deeply to tether him when there was little to no chance of things working out between them.

The hardest thing she'd ever done had been to let him go. The next hardest had been to bury her father. And that alone spoke volumes of how much she'd once loved Isaac Richards.

The burning question, and one she wasn't sure she wanted to know the answer to, was did she still love him?

She had a horrible suspicion that she did.

'Did you see the sparks flying between those two?' Petra asked Harry, as soon as Isaac and Nelly left, Amos and Nathan hot on their heels – Amos had dinner to prepare, and Nathan muttered something about fetching the ponies in from the field. She got heavily to her feet and began to collect up the mugs.

'I'll do that.' Harry came up behind her and wrapped his arms around her, cradling her stomach.

Petra leant back into him, feeling his solid chest against her aching back. Thirty weeks pregnant meant she still had two long months to go before their baby put in an appearance.

'They've definitely got history,' she mused. 'I wonder what it is.'

'As long as it doesn't affect the build, I don't care,' Harry said.

'Where's your sense of romance?'

Harry snorted. 'I never thought I'd hear the word **romance** coming from you. Remember when we first met? I don't think you knew what it meant.'

Petra tilted her head to the side so he could nuzzle her neck. 'Mmm, that's nice.' The baby seemed to like it too because he kicked vigorously. 'Did you feel that?'

 Harry's voice was full of wonder. 'I most certainly did. He's a strong little blighter, isn't he?'

'Tell me about it. You ought to try being on the receiving end.'

'I would if I could,' he said, and she twisted around in his arms to face him.

'I know,' she replied softly, her arms around his neck.

He wanted this baby so much and he loved her so completely, that it took her breath away every time she thought about it.

What a change a year had brought to her life, she mused, as she gazed into his eyes and saw her love reflected in their depths. When she'd first met Harry, never in a million years would she have believed she could have gone from mistrustful animosity to loving him with every cell in her body.

He bent his head and kissed her gently, and the baby kicked again.

'Ow! Someone's jealous,' she said, and Harry grinned down at her.

'Someone is going to have to get used to his daddy kissing his mummy, because I've no intention of stopping.'

'We'll just have to wait until he's asleep,' Petra said.

'No, we won't! I want him to know how much I love you. It'll be good for him to see that his parents adore each other.'

'Oh, so you think I adore you, do you?' she teased, her mouth on his.

'You'd better, Mrs Milton, because **I** adore **you**.'

'I'm not Mrs Milton yet.'

'You soon will be. Have you found a dress you like?'

Petra pulled back and looked at her stomach. 'How can I when this is expanding faster than the damned universe? I need a marquee, not a wedding dress. No, I'm going to wait until after the baby is born and see what I can fit into.'

'Are you sure you don't want to sneak off to the registry office? We could be married in as little as three weeks,' Harry suggested.

'Are you that keen to get hitched?'

'Yes.' He nodded emphatically.

'That's so sweet.'

'I'm not sweet. I'm rough and rugged,' he objected in mock indignation.

'You're a total softie...'

'Sorry to interrupt,' Amos said, from the doorway. 'But you've got a class in half an hour.'

'So I have,' Petra said. 'I'd better give Nathan a hand bringing the ponies up from the field.'

'Do you want any help?' Harry asked.

'I've got this, but if you could ask Timothy when he's free? We've got a cow shed to clear.'

Wedding dresses and cow sheds practically in the same sentence? Petra smiled as she walked down the lane a few moments later, a couple of lead ropes in her hands. Running a riding school was hardly glamorous!

Nathan was unbolting the gate to the field when he saw her approach, and he waited for her to catch up. 'I think something is going on between your architect and your builder,' he said, holding the gate open for her.

'You noticed, too?'

'It was hard not to.'

'I wonder if they've worked together before?'

'Maybe, but didn't you say she owns a local firm and he's come from away?' Nathan asked.

'Yeah, Nelly owns Ken Newsome Building Contractors. They've got a good reputation. Her father started the business and built it up. Nelly took over from him when he died.'

'Do you trust her to do a good job?'

Petra bristled. 'I hope you're not implying that a female builder isn't as good as a man?'

Nathan gave her a sideways look. 'I wouldn't dare. I was talking about the way she reacted to your architect when she saw him. And he looked just as... I'm not sure how you'd describe it.'

Petra grinned. 'Hungry? Isaac looked at her like he was starving and she was a three-course meal.'

'You've hit the nail on the head,' he said, moving further into the field, Petra accompanying him, her eyes picking out the ponies they needed to catch for this afternoon's lesson.

If Isaac and Nelly's first meeting was any indication, the next few months were going to be interesting.

CHAPTER TWO

There were two stages to every build that Nelly particularly enjoyed – the beginning where she worked out the intricacies of the project, and the end where everyone's efforts were finally realised. The in between bit was pure hard work and frequently littered with problems. In her experience, it was rare for a build to run smoothly, to run to time and to come in on budget.

As she stood inside the cow shed, an iPad in her hand, Nelly was in her element. Planning a project was a complex activity involving detailed notes, meticulous attention to detail and a task sheet as long as her arm, but she loved it.

This morning she was on site trying to estimate how long each stage of the build would take so she could calendar in when she needed sub-contractors, such as the electricians, to do their bit. In her experience, each phase overlapped and often needed a certain degree of fluidity. It was challenging and demanding work, but that's why she enjoyed it so much. It might be difficult to envisage the finished product when standing in the middle of a dark and dirty stone-built barn that still smelt faintly of cow poo, but as she wandered around using a digital copy of the plans that Isaac had supplied, she could see the transformation taking place in her mind.

That massive stone trough? That was where one of the kitchens would be located. That wall over there would have three holes punched through it for windows. The corrugated iron sheeting on the roof? Replaced with new rafters and smooth grey slate, with solar panels to generate at least 50 per cent of the electricity the cottages would use.

Nelly added another item to her ever-growing list – ask Petra who was sourcing the panels. The stables' owners weren't employing a separate project manager, but were going to oversee the build themselves, which was a mistake in Nelly's opinion. Unless clients had experience in that field, it was going to be a steep learning curve for them. Petra especially, because Nelly had the feeling that it would be Petra who was going to be the person most involved in the decision-making and in driving the project forward.

And the woman was about seven months pregnant!

Nelly had to admire her. It wasn't going to be easy.

As she scribbled on the tablet, Nelly thought back to yesterday, when she'd met their architect for the first time. But it hadn't been the first time, had it? Her heart gave a jolt as she thought about Isaac. It had been doing that a lot over the last twenty or so hours. She wished she didn't have to think about him, but it was going to be hard not to since she would be working closely with him.

A line from an old black and white film flitted through her mind... "of all the gin joints in all the towns in all the world..."

he'd walked into hers. Was it fate that their paths had crossed again? Or simply an unfortunate set of circumstances?

Considering the line of work they were both in, it might seem inevitable that they would bump into each other at some point, except for one thing – Nelly lived in Picklewick, and Isaac didn't. The last she'd heard, he was in Wiltshire and she wondered what he was doing here.

'Hello?' The unexpected sound of Petra's voice made Nelly squeak in surprise and whirl around.

'Sorry, I didn't mean to startle you,' Petra said. 'I saw your van and thought I'd check that everything was okay.' She was silhouetted in one of the doorways, a dark figure against the bright May morning outside.

Nelly put a hand to her thudding heart. 'I was in a world of my own,' she explained.

Petra walked towards her. 'As you can see, we've not begun yet,' she said, almost apologetically.

'I've come to write a plan of action,' Nelly said. 'A tentative one,' she added. 'How soon I can implement it depends on when I can start.'

Petra grinned at her. 'We've got a clearing party arranged for this weekend. You're welcome to come along.'

Nelly hesitated, not sure how she should respond considering that her clients had informed her they wanted to do this part of the build themselves to try to keep costs down. Had they changed their minds, or were they expecting her to work for free?

Maybe Petra read her mind because she added, 'Amos is firing up the barbeque, so you're welcome to pop in for a burger and a beer. No obligation: we don't expect you to put your hard hat on and join in, especially since this bit isn't part of your contract.'

'Thanks, I might drop by. I'll have to see how it goes,' Nelly said, relieved that was cleared up. She hadn't wanted to be rude and ask for clarification, but some bad experiences with a couple of clients she'd worked with in the past had taught her to be wary. Nelly was running a business not a charity, and even though she always wanted to do as much as she could to help her clients, working for free wasn't a good business model: the bank wouldn't be pleased for one thing, and for another she had her staff's wages to pay.

Anyway, however kind Petra's offer was, Nelly had no intention of dropping in because she knew she wouldn't be able to resist getting her hands dirty and joining in.

Which reminded her... 'You need to wear a hard hat from now on when you're on site,' Nelly said. She tapped her own.

'I've got a riding helmet. Will that do?'

'Probably, but be prepared for it to get ruined. Knocking things down and building them back up is a dirty business.'

Petra laughed. 'These hats aren't the fancy sort that you see on The Horse of the Year Show,' she said. 'You're thinking of the ones covered in velvet. The helmet I wear is a bog-standard fibreglass one – no fabric of any description.'

'I see.' Nelly didn't know the first thing about riding hats; or about horses, for that matter.

'Do you ride?' Petra asked.

'Regretfully not.' Horse riding hadn't appealed to her, unlike some of her friends who had been mad about ponies.

'Have you ever ridden?'

'Does a donkey ride on the beach count?'

Petra chuckled. 'It's a start. Would you like to learn?'

Nelly wasn't sure. She tended to prefer mechanical rides such as diggers, rather than horsey ones, and she made a see-saw motion with her hand, not wanting to offend her newest client.

'You're going to be here for a couple of months, so let me show you around,' Petra offered.

Nelly raised her eyebrows. 'This build is going to take more than a couple of months. You'll be lucky if it's completed in four. Even six would be pushing it.'

'I'm sure you'll give it your best shot,' Petra said airily. 'Come on, I've got a donkey to show you, and a stubborn pregnant goat.'

Isaac leaned back in his chair and rolled his head, wincing at the crunch in his neck. His shoulders were tense and his eyes felt gritty, which wasn't surprising considering his lack of sleep last night.

He'd driven away from the stables on Muddypuddle Lane with his senses filled with Nelly – the sight of her, the sound of her voice, the scent of the perfume he'd caught wisps of and had recognised instantly as one she used to wear when she could afford it. He'd bought her a bottle once for her birthday. The smell of it had swept over and through him, affecting him even more than seeing her had done. Even his skin had tingled as he remembered how she had felt in his arms, how soft she'd been, how demanding.

Oh dear, best not to go there. Seeing her so unexpectedly was bad enough, but allowing memories of delicious nights spent in each other's student bed was a step too far. If he was going to work with her (which he had no choice about) he must put their past to the back of his mind and keep it there.

Isaac swivelled in his chair and peered out of the window. His office consisted of a small suite of rooms (three to be precise) in a block of similar suites, which he was currently renting until he found a more permanent base. Leaving Wiltshire hadn't been the easiest of decisions to make, especially since he'd made a bit of a name for himself there as a decent architect, but needs must, and the needs of his mum had called him back. Dad leaving had sent her into a tailspin and Isaac wanted to be there to support her. He had no idea what had happened between his parents to end their thirty-seven-year marriage because neither of them would say anything other than they'd grown apart, but clearly it must be something drastic because his mum was inconsolable and his father was tight-lipped and defensive.

All Isaac could do was to be there for them, his mum in particular because she appeared to be coping less well with the split.

It had been a wrench leaving Wiltshire, but he was self-employed and he could relocate his business to anywhere he wanted. He had a professional website, with an impressive array of testimonials which was easily transportable, and in the four months since he'd returned to the area he'd grown up in, he'd managed to land a decent number of clients.

When he thought about it logically, he was surprised he hadn't bumped into Nelly before now, considering they were both in the same line of work and Picklewick was only about nine miles away. However, in his defence, he'd deliberately **not** thought about her. He'd spent the last thirteen years **not** thinking about her.

During those first horrible months when he had been forced to come to terms with the fact that she hadn't loved him as much as he'd loved her, he'd obsessively searched for any and all mentions of her and her dad's business online, but there hadn't been a great deal to be found. From what Nelly had told him, Ken had been a word-of-mouth type of builder, listed on yell.com but that was about it – no website, no Facebook account, nothing, and Nelly had also disappeared into the void as though she'd never existed.

As the months had turned into years, Isaac had begun to wonder if he'd imagined her, to ask himself if she really had existed. If it hadn't been for the hole she'd left in his heart, he might have believed he'd dreamt her.

When the initial acute pain of her leaving had eventually subsided to an ache he could live with without it being so debilitating that it crushed him during every waking hour, he'd put her in a box in his head and had hidden it in the depths of his mind. And there it had stayed (more or less), until yesterday, when his personal Pandora's box had been well and truly opened.

Taking a glance at the drawings he was supposed to be working on, Isaac let out a heartfelt sigh. He should try to concentrate on his work, but his wayward thoughts kept leading him back to Nelly.

He honestly wasn't sure how he felt about her. The attraction was still very much in evidence – she had become a beautiful woman – but was that the only emotion he was feeling?

Isaac blew out his cheeks. No, he didn't think so. What he was feeling was an undeniable resurrection of the ache in his heart that he'd long since thought he'd cured. But was the ache a rekindling of his old feelings, or was it nostalgia for a time when life was less complicated and he didn't have to adult? On looking back, life had been so much simpler then, even though it hadn't felt like it at the time. It had also been monochrome, with things either black or white. Shades of grey hadn't entered his world at that point, and when Nelly had dropped out of the course, left uni and had gone home, he'd interpreted it as her not loving him any more. Now, though he understood that she probably **had** loved him – just not enough to stay with him when life had got in the way.

He rolled his head once more, the tension easing slightly.

Maybe what he'd felt had been the intense emotions of first love, and everyone had their hearts broken sooner or later – unless they married their first loves, of course.

Speaking of marriage, he hadn't seen a ring on her finger but that didn't mean to say she didn't have a partner. Or that she didn't remove it when she was working, because rings could get caught, and building work was tough and physical.

Telling himself it was mere curiosity and nothing more, Isaac turned back to his computer and opened a new tab in the search engine and typed in her name.

A half an hour later and he was still none the wiser, and although there didn't appear to be any evidence of a man in her life, Isaac couldn't definitely say there wasn't.

Cross with himself for wasting time when he should be working, he shut the tab down and told himself to focus on what was important.

But the thought kept niggling away at him that Nelly's relationship status was very important indeed, and a part of him began to harbour the smallest of hopes that he and Nelly might be able to get to know each other all over again. Because, for him, the spark was still there, whether he wanted it to be or not.

'Have you and Isaac worked together before?' Petra asked.

She and Nelly were standing in what Petra had called "the tack room" where the saddles and bridles were kept. It smelled strongly of horse and leather. Nelly didn't find it an unpleasant smell, but she preferred the aroma of cement, if she was honest. Each to their own...

The tour of the stables had been nice though, especially when she got to stroke the long soft ears of a donkey, and she never knew that ponies' noses were so soft and nibbley. There had been fluffy chicks too, which were simply the cutest things ever.

Nelly and Petra each had a mug of tea in their hands and there was an open packet of Ginger Nut biscuits on the shelf next to the kettle, which Petra was busily munching her way through.

'Not really. We were in university together,' Nelly replied.

'What did you study?'

'Architecture.'

'I didn't realise you were an architect as well as a builder?'

Nelly pulled a face. 'I'm not. I dropped out halfway through my second year. My dad was ill and he needed someone to run the business for a while. I always intended to go back and finish the course, but Dad didn't get better, so...'

'You ended up running the company permanently?' Petra finished.

Nelly nodded. It sounded way easier and more straightforward than it had actually been. She'd dropped out of the course, meaning to pick it up again the following year, but it hadn't happened.

She'd also dropped out of something else – her relationship with Isaac.

Picking that up again would have been nigh on impossible. Everyone knew long distance love didn't work. Besides, they were both students, for god's sake – it wasn't meant to have been serious. But it had been, for her at least; and she'd got the feeling that Isaac had been just as heart-broken when she'd called it off. She wished she hadn't had to, but she'd had no choice – and she'd loved him too deeply and too fiercely to try to hang onto him.

She had set him free to get on with his life, and although she'd been heartbroken it had been the right thing to do. No doubt he had soon got over her.

Nelly wondered how he'd lived that life. Was he married? Did he have kids? Did he ever think about her?

Forget that last bit – she hoped he didn't, because she'd thought about him constantly for months and it had hurt so much. She wouldn't wish that kind of pain on her greatest enemy, and certainly not on the man she'd loved with all her heart, the man who she'd once hoped was The One.

She had yet to find anyone she wanted to spend the rest of her life with, because she hadn't experienced love like that since.

'You've done a good job of running it,' Petra said, bringing Nelly back to the present. 'When Harry was asking around for recommendations for local builders, Ken Newsome's name kept coming up, along with "don't be put off because Ken isn't a bloke". Your company has got a damned good reputation.'

'Glad to hear it,' Nelly said mildly.

Petra was giving her an assessing look. 'It couldn't have been easy.'

Nelly's gaze was level. 'It wasn't.'

There was silence for a few moments, then Petra said, 'You'll do.'

'Thanks!' Nelly chuckled.

'I bet you've had to work twice as hard and be twice as good as any bloke.'

'You've got that right.' Nelly had lost count of the number of times she'd answered the phone to a potential customer, only for the person on the other end to assume she was the office girl, especially in the early days when she had been so young.

It used to gall her that people equated youth with inexperience. She'd grown up with a father who used to take her with him when he went on a job. She'd been able to lay a course of house bricks before she'd been able to tie her shoelaces. Concrete blocks had come later, when she'd had the strength to lift them. Her dad had taught her about self-levelling concrete, lintels, the safest way to knock down a wall, the right sort of sand to use.

He'd taught her everything she knew, and he'd never been as proud as when she'd told him she wanted to be an architect. The plan had been for her to design it and for him to build it. They would have made a great team. But then he developed a pain in his back which he put down to a strain, and he had a cough that he'd ignored for far too long.

Now here she was, running one of the best firms of building contractors for miles around. Her dad had been proud of her right to the end.

CHAPTER THREE

'Timothy!' Harry cried, slapping his younger brother on the back and almost sending him flying. 'It's about time you did some manual labour.' Timothy and his girlfriend Charity were the first to arrive for the "clearing weekend". It was fortuitous that Timothy wasn't on call today because clearing the cow shed was going to be a mammoth job, Harry realised.

Timothy rose to his full height and bristled. 'I'll have you know that being a vet involves a great deal of manual labour.'

Harry winked at Charity, who said, 'Stand down, Timmo, he's having you on.'

'**Timmo**?' Harry chuckled. 'Is that your pet name for him?'

Charity smirked. 'Only when he's being a prat.'

'Being a prat, am I?' Timothy made to leave, shaking his head. 'And here I was, about to give up my valuable free time to help you guys out.'

'Did you have anything else lined up?' Petra asked.

'Yeah, sleeping,' was Timothy's reply, as he bent to give her a kiss on the cheek.

'You can sleep later,' she told him. 'Harry needs you.'

'After the comment he just made, Harry can go boil his head,' Timothy joked. 'I'm here for **you**, not for him. Have you managed to rope any other idiots in, or is it just me and Harry who will be doing all the hard work?'

'See, I told you he was scared of a bit of hard graft,' Harry said, dodging out of the way as Timothy aimed a playful punch at him.

'What am I? Decoration?' Charity demanded. 'I'm perfectly capable of hauling stuff around.' She looked positively put out at the implication.

'Don't let our builder hear you say that,' Petra said to Timothy. 'Just to give you a heads-up, she's female and she won't take kindly to you implying that she's not as capable as a man.'

Timothy looked horrified. 'I wouldn't dream of it.'

Harry thought it best to step in before his brother had both Petra and Charity on his back. 'I'd quit now, while you're still upright,' he advised. 'Have you **seen** Charity lift a bale of hay? **You're** more likely to be the decoration around here.'

'I can't help it if I'm pretty,' Timothy quipped, earning himself a round of rolled eyes and groans.

Harry grinned. Today might very well be hard work, but it also promised to be fun, especially with Amos manning the barbeque from lunchtime onwards and the promise of cold beers and a gorgeously sunny day. All he hoped was that he could keep Petra in check, because he knew she'd be wanting to get stuck in and do her bit. He'd have to box clever so that she didn't get on her high horse and give him the "I'm pregnant, not ill" speech. His fiancée was as bossy as they came, so he'd appeal to that side of her nature and try to persuade her to do the supervising. They still had to work out where all the stuff they were taking out of the cow shed was going to go, for a start.

He was still mulling the problem over when Nathan arrived with Megan, quickly followed by October's mum, Lena, who had been driven to the stables by Luca, October's boyfriend.

Harry had expected to see Nathan, but not his partner Megan, and he greeted them both with enthusiasm and gratitude.

'I thought Amos could do with a hand keeping the troops fed and watered,' Megan said.

Lena was also a surprise. 'I might not be able to do any heavy lifting, but I'm pretty good at clearing up,' she announced. 'Besides, I can always help out with the catering side of things too, and I know October won't be around all day as she's taking a hack out, so I thought you could do with all the help you can get.'

'That's very kind of you,' he said, touched, and when he glanced at Petra he could see that she was equally moved.

'I'm here all day,' Luca said. 'Just tell me what you want me to do.'

Harry was about to round everyone up and head over to the cow shed where Amos had already rolled out the barbeque, when another car trundled up the lane.

When it came to a halt and William Reid got out, Harry's eyes widened. He hadn't expected the manager of Picklewick's care home to pay them a visit this morning, and he wondered what the man wanted.

William saw Harry looking and he shouted over, 'Come and give me a hand with this, will you?'

"This" turned out to be a large silver-coloured urn, which would make several hundred cups of tea by the look of it.

'I thought it would come in handy, rather than boiling a kettle every five minutes,' William said, and Harry saw Megan's eyes light up. It would certainly make providing hot drinks easier.

'Thank you so much!' Harry exclaimed, feeling a lump in his throat at everyone's thoughtfulness and willingness to help. Petra turned away blinking furiously, and he guessed she was just as affected as he.

Back in January, when he'd had the idea to transform the cow shed into holiday lets, it had been a pie-in-the-sky dream, and he hadn't truly believed it would happen. There had been so many obstacles – the main one being the cost – that he hadn't thought it had a hope in hell of becoming a reality, despite him offering to plough the capital he'd received as his half of the sale of his parents' house (Timothy was in the process of using his share to buy the cottage he and Charity were living in). If it wasn't for Petra agreeing to be his wife and his insistence that once they were married what was his would also become hers, Harry didn't think Petra would have considered the venture. He just hoped that once the renovations were done and once the cow shed had been magically transformed into three holiday cottages, the stables would be able to turn a profit without his wife-to-be having to work all the hours God sends.

He was looking forward to spending as much time as possible with his wife and child, and it would be tough to run two businesses with a newborn to look after, although he might consider dropping his farrier business down to part-time in order to help Petra more. So he was hoping that the additional income from the holiday lets would allow her to employ someone else, enabling her to take a step back.

With so many people turning up to help with the preparatory work on the cow shed, the building work could start soon. It might be unrealistic of him, but he was hoping the bulk of it would be over by Petra's due date.

He had so much to look forward to over the next few months – a complete renovation project, a new baby and a wedding. Talk about not doing things by halves!

Amos wasn't ready to fire up the barbeque yet, but at least it was in position: Harry had helped drag it over from their enclosed garden at the rear of the house and position it near the shed. Actually, Harry had done most of the dragging and lifting where necessary, with Amos supervising.

Amos was busy checking the charcoal situation, while also keeping a beady eye on the weather, when he heard a gaggle of voices.

What on earth...? Putting the bag of woodchips down, which he'd planned on adding to the coals once they were lit, Amos stood with his hands on his hips and waited.

Within a few seconds, a group of eight people came around the corner, closely followed by Harry and William Reid from the care home in the village who were carrying what looked like a large urn between them.

Amos blinked. 'Is that an urn?'

'Yep. Have you got a power source?' William asked, puffing slightly as they shuffled it around and stood it on top of one of the tables which had been set up.

'Er, yes. There's an extension cable over there.' Amos pointed. He was running a lead from the barn in order to boil the kettle, but an urn was a much better idea.

'Got any jugs?' Megan asked, flexing her arms.

'Hi, Megan, I didn't expect to see you. Or you, Lena. How's your mum?' Amos enquired.

'So, so. But thanks for asking.'

'Are you all here to help?' he asked, confused.

'We most certainly are,' Megan said. 'More hands make light work. Now, have you got any jugs?' she repeated. 'The sooner we fill this urn, the sooner we can all have a brew.'

Amos watched Megan and Lena get to work with calm efficiency and he shook his head, bemused and more than a little grateful.

He knew Megan fairly well, even though she'd only been coming to the stables for about six months and had been with Nathan for less than that. She and Nathan had got together while Megan had been working her way through a series of letters that her deceased husband had left her. His last one had informed her he'd booked horse-riding lessons for her. It had been his final gift, a gift designed to set her free of her mourning and give her a chance to live again. It had worked – Nathan had fallen in love with her and she with him, and now they were practically inseparable.

She'd also brought cake. Lots and lots of cake. Megan had recently set up a cake-decorating business and Amos's mouth watered in anticipation at the sweet treats.

Lena, on the other hand, was a total surprise. He'd known Lena for years, but hadn't had a great deal to do with her. She'd moved to Picklewick about ten years ago when her mother, Olive, who'd recently had to go into a care home, needed help. He often saw Olive when he visited the care home, and he sometimes bumped into Lena too, but he hadn't expected to see her at the stables. He didn't think she particularly liked horses, for one thing, despite her daughter,

October, being a first-class rider and a very competent groom.

While he was fetching mugs from the kitchen and digging out the paper plates he'd bought especially for today, Amos kept glancing over at her. For some reason she reminded him of Mags, his wife. Lord, how he missed her. She'd been gone a fair few years, but her loss wasn't any easier to handle now than it had been in those awful weeks and months after she'd died. The one saving grace to come out of his wife's passing was that he'd got to know his niece much better than he otherwise might have done. So well, that he'd asked Petra to move in with him and help run the stables. It had been a dream come true for her and a godsend for him, because he didn't know how he would have managed without her, especially after his angina diagnosis.

His gaze drifted to her, and he noted with satisfaction that she wasn't attempting to lift or move anything herself, but was busy directing everyone else. They might call it being bossy, but they took it in good cheer, and someone had even rigged up some speakers to their phone and dance music accompanied the laughter and the chatter.

This is a good day, Amos thought, and these were good people. He was lucky to have so many friends who were willing to help, and a family who loved him. Of the people helping with this new and exciting phase in the life of the stables, he might technically only be related to Petra, but he viewed both Harry and Nathan as surrogate sons, and soon there would be a baby to love and cherish.

With a deep feeling of gratitude, Amos set about firing up the barbeque. Very soon he'd have hungry mouths to feed.

Isaac hadn't intended to go anywhere near the stables on Muddypuddle Lane today, but for some reason he found himself driving up the rutted track this afternoon, his car bumping over the potholes, before his brain had caught up with what the rest of his body was doing.

Telling himself that as he was here now, he may as well show his face, he parked his car in the carpark (which was nearly as pitted and potholed as the lane) and got out, inhaling the unmistakable aroma of horse, overlaid by a mouth-watering smell of charcoaled meat and frying onions.

He'd stay long enough to make sure they weren't knocking down a wall they shouldn't, he'd have a burger if there was one on offer, then he'd skedaddle. He didn't want to risk being asked to shift or lift anything. That job was down to the clients and the builder.

The builder...Isaac wondered if Nelly would be here, and he scanned the parked vehicles but none of them had Ken Newsome's name emblazoned on the side.

He wasn't sure whether to be relieved or disappointed.

After changing into the steel toecap work boots that he always kept in the car and grabbing his hard hat, he followed the sounds of music, laughter and the clang of metal. As soon as he rounded the side

of the barn he came face-to-face with
Petra.

'Isaac! Nice to see you!' Petra was filthy,
covered from head to foot in a coating of
fine dust. Incongruously, she was wearing
a pair of dungarees that stretched across
her rounded belly, a riding hat, and a pair
of bright pink wellies with navy flowers on
them. At least, he thought they were pink
– it was difficult to tell through all the
grime.

'How are you getting on?' he asked.

'Come and see for yourself.'

Praying that they hadn't demolished
something they shouldn't have, he walked
slowly towards the shed, plonking his
hard hat on his head.

'Have you come to give us a hand?' Harry called when he saw him, and Isaac shook his head and laughed.

'I've come for a beer and a burger,' he called back.

Harry gave him a thumbs-up. Harry and three other men were trying to manoeuvre the massive stone trough onto the tines of a tractor. Nathan was at the tractor's helm, and Isaac watched in fascination as Nathan delicately inserted the tines underneath the trough, and the stone edifice began to rise.

'Everyone move back!' Harry shouted, as the tractor trundled slowly out of the shed. He dusted his hands off and came to join Isaac and Petra, who were standing a safe distance away. The farrier was as grimy as his fiancée, but he had a huge grin on his face.

'The shed is almost clear, I see,' Isaac said. 'I can't believe you've done so much in such a short space of time.'

The cow shed had little else in it now, apart from the partitions which would have to come down at some point, but even with them still in place, he was finally able to fully appreciate how big the area was. The building would make three airy and spacious cottages.

'It's all Petra's doing – she's a real slave driver,' Harry chuckled, turning to the three men who'd been helping with the trough. 'Sorry, I haven't introduced you. This is Timothy, my brother. He's one of the local vets. This is Luca, October's other half – he's got a horse stabled here. And last but not least is William, who manages Picklewick's care home.'

With the introductions made, everyone headed outside and made their way over to the barbeque area, stopping off at an outside tap to wash their hands. Isaac got in line and rinsed his hands. It was as he turned to where Amos had set up the food that he spotted Nelly.

His stomach flipped and his heart stuttered. Appetite suddenly vanished, he wondered whether he should say his goodbyes and leave. He'd been half-expecting her (that **was** why you're here, a treacherous little voice in his mind pointed out) but faced with the reality of her, Isaac suddenly wanted to run. Or scoop her up in his arms and kiss her soundly. He couldn't quite decide which.

It didn't help that she was looking absolutely delectable. When he'd seen her the other day in Amos's dining room she'd been wearing jeans and a sweatshirt, with chunky work boots on her feet. Today though...oh, my goodness. Her pale blue dress clung to her waist and flared out over her hips, she was wearing sandals that revealed pink-painted toes, and her legs were bare. Her hair curled on her shoulders, and she had sunglasses perched on the top of her head.

Nelly Newsome hadn't come to the stables to lend a hand, that much was clear.

And she wasn't dressed for entering a building site either.

So why **was** she here? To offer moral support? Because she fancied some charred meat on a skewer? Or was she here because she hoped he might be?

It was a heady thought, and one he dismissed as soon as it occurred to him. **Of course** her presence had nothing to do with him. Why would it?

She might even be here with someone – a significant other.

Surreptitiously Isaac glanced around, coming to the conclusion that if she was here with a man, the only one it could possibly be was William. It set his teeth on edge to think they might be a couple and an unexpected bolt of pure, unadulterated jealously struck him in the chest.

Dry-mouthed and reluctant, he caught her eye and nodded.

Nelly nodded back, her expression giving nothing away. He couldn't tell whether she was pleased to see him, annoyed, or completely uninterested.

To his dismay he was extraordinarily pleased to see her – and that wasn't good. Not good at all.

Nelly's pulse hammered in her throat and she put a hand to her chest, trying to ease the sudden clamouring of her heart. She could feel a blush spreading across her cheeks and she willed it away. Seeing Isaac at the build wasn't unexpected, so why was she reacting like this?

Undoubtedly he was here for the same reason she was – to make sure the clients weren't too over enthusiastic in their clearing of the site. From the way he was dressed, he didn't appear to want to take part in the event either. His jeans were newish, and he was wearing a white tee shirt and trainers. His only concession to being on a building site was the hard hat he was holding. Nelly had hers in her voluminous handbag. She didn't intend putting it on until she went inside the shed because, let's face it, summer dresses and sandals didn't go with hard hats and work boots. She'd brought a pair of those with her too, and they were currently sitting next to one of the chairs that had been appropriated from the arena's viewing gallery and set up near the food.

By wearing a pretty dress and sandals, she wanted to make it clear to her clients that she wasn't here to work, but to give them some support.

Yeah, right... Ignoring her suspicion that the dress was purely for Isaac's benefit (as was the make-up and the freshly washed hair), and also refusing to acknowledge that she was here more in the hope of bumping into Isaac than for customer relations, Nelly accepted a burger from Amos, grabbed a bottle of non-alcoholic beer and took a seat.

Petra quickly joined her. 'I hate this,' she said, holding up a non-alcoholic beer of her own and giving Harry an evil stare. He was drinking the real stuff, Nelly noticed.

'You've got a little one to think of,' Nelly said. 'How long do you have to go?'

'Eight weeks.' Petra's tone of voice made Nelly laugh.

'Come and talk to me when **you're** seven months pregnant,' Petra moaned. 'I bet you won't be laughing about it then.' She pulled a face. 'I feel as though I'm carting a small horse around in here.' She brightened. 'And I'm not the only one expecting to hear the patter of tiny feet. Remember Princess the goat? She's due to give birth any day now.'

'Crumbs, it's all go, isn't it?'

'I love spring,' Petra said, taking a swig of her beer and grimacing. 'All the new growth and the new life. It's my favourite time of the year.'

'And a new build,' Nelly said. 'Here's to it going well. Which it will,' she added, clinking bottles with Petra. 'Do you mind if I take a look inside?'

'Want to make sure we haven't demolished anything vital?' Petra quipped. 'It's okay, Isaac has already checked, but you're welcome to see for yourself. Anyway, you're soon going to be spending more time in there than anyone else, so you might as well make yourself at home.'

Nelly slipped her feet into her work boots, her toes feeling naked without socks, and popped her hard hat on.

Petra tilted her head to one side. 'Can I just say that neither the boots nor the hat go with the dress.' She paused, then added, 'Would you like me to ask Isaac to go inside with you? I'm assuming you are usually in close contact with the architect on a build like this?' She looked innocent and wide-eyed, but Nelly frowned.

Had Petra realised that she had feelings for Isaac? Nelly hoped not. It was bad enough that she had them at all, without other people being aware of it.

Oh, hell! An unpleasant thought occurred to her. If Petra had noticed, might Isaac have noticed, too?

Embarrassment made her ears burn and she was glad her hat covered them. Bright red ear-tips had always been a sign that she was discomforted, and although Isaac had probably forgotten that little quirk of hers, she didn't want to take any chances that he might realise she was disconcerted.

'I'm fine on my own,' she said, noticing that he was occupied with a burger. Feeling reasonably certain she was safe to go into the shed without bumping into him, she put her food down on the table, took a swig of her beer and wandered casually off in the direction of the cow shed.

Wow, they'd done a fantastic amount of work, she saw. The place was empty apart from the dust motes swirling in the air, making her sneeze.

'I believe they are tackling the floor tomorrow,' Isaac said from behind, and Nelly jumped.

'I didn't expect to see you here,' she replied, without turning around.

'I didn't expect to see you, either. I thought you'd have had enough of building sites, without visiting one on your day off.'

'I only came for the free food. It'll save me cooking later.'

Nelly heard Isaac move closer and suddenly he was standing beside her, so close she could smell him. Mmm... She swallowed: her mouth was dry and her lips felt wooden. She knew that smell so well, and it set her heart thudding and the blood rushing through her veins.

Damn him! He could at least smell different. It was bad enough seeing him and hearing him, without the familiar and evocative scent of him wafting up her nose. All she needed to complete the hat trick was to kiss him, so she could taste him and feel him as well.

Woah there, girlie, she said to herself. Had the thought of kissing him really slipped into her mind? What a wally. She needed to get ideas like that out of her head, pronto. He was here to do a job, and so was she. The last thing she needed (or her clients needed, for that matter) was for her to drool over their architect. Isaac probably wouldn't be too pleased, either. For all she knew, he had a wife or a girlfriend who wouldn't appreciate an ex showing an interest.

Not only that, thirteen years was a long time. She should be over him by now.

Hell, she'd thought she was, until she'd seen him in her client's dining room, as large as life and twice as handsome.

Gosh, he really **was** handsome. The years had taken his boyish good looks and turned them into something more mature, and she felt the force of his presence like a hammer to her soul.

Briefly she closed her eyes, wishing that things had been different. If only her dad—

No! She refused to think like that. What had happened, had happened. She'd do it again in a heartbeat. Her coming back home and taking up the reins of the family business had made her dad's passing easier for him. She could no more wish that away than she could wish that Isaac still loved her.

And it was then that she knew without a shadow of a doubt that she still loved him. She always had, and she suspected she always would. More's the pity, because she now faced several months of working with him.

Stifling a cry, Nelly whirled on her heel. 'Sorry, there's somewhere I need to be,' she said abruptly. Then she fled.

She might have to work with him, but the ordeal didn't have to start now. All she wanted to do was to go home and try to forget Isaac Richards existed.

CHAPTER FOUR

Amos sighed theatrically and reached for a towel to wipe his hands. Why was it that whenever he had his hands in a bowl of water, the phone rang? He'd been about to wash the kitchen cupboards down because they hadn't been done for ages and he didn't want Petra to look at them and get the idea that she should give them a clean – his niece had more than enough to be going on with. The least he could do was uphold his part of the bargain and keep the house in order, so that she didn't feel she had to.

Expecting it to be a parent wanting to book, amend, or cancel their child's riding lesson, he hurried to answer it.

'Amos? It's Sandra from the HRC. I don't know if you remember me? We met at the agricultural show last year.'

Amos thought for a moment, racking his brains. Got her! She ran a horse charity which rescued and rehomed abused, abandoned and neglected horses.

'I remember,' he said, hoping she wasn't calling to tap him up for a donation. With the cow shed conversion going ahead, the stables needed every penny they could lay their hands on, despite Harry's very generous insertion of funds. Harry might soon be Petra's husband and had argued that what was his was hers, but Amos was keenly aware that it was the money Harry had got from the sale of his deceased parents' house that was paying for the project.

'What can I do for you?' he asked, warily.

'A huge favour, I hope.'

Amos's heart sank.

He was about to say that they weren't in a position to donate, when Sandra continued, 'Can you take a horse? I wouldn't normally ask, but she's in a bit of a state and is heavily pregnant. She's about to drop any day now and I can't risk moving her too far. We're full to bursting and can't take another animal, and the next nearest centre is over fifty miles away. I'm scared she'll go into labour on route.'

Amos hesitated. They had enough to go on with themselves, what with the clearing party on the weekend and the building work starting shortly after. The stables on Muddypuddle Lane was hardly going to be a haven of tranquillity over the coming weeks, and not only that, it sounded as though the mare might need a great deal of care and attention.

But then Sandra said something that made him sit up and take notice. 'She's producing colostrum.'

That changed everything. If the mare's teats had started secreting colostrum it meant that labour was imminent.

'How soon can you get her to us?' he asked.

'Within the hour.'

'We'll have a stall ready for her.'

'I can't thank you enough,' Sandra said, the relief in her voice evident.

As soon as she rang off, Amos hastened to find Nathan. It looked like the stables would soon hear the patter of tiny horsey hooves and, despite the amount of extra work it would cause, he found he was incredibly excited at the prospect of having a newborn foal to care for.

'All right, love?' Nelly's mum greeted her as she opened the front door and led her into the lounge. Jayne had been reading one of the crime novels she loved and enjoying a glass of wine.

'Where's Reggie?' Nelly asked. Reggie was her step-dad, and although Nelly was pleased that her mum had found love again after Dad died, it had taken her a while to accept him. Thankfully, Jayne had moved in with Reggie and not the other way around, so Nelly was spared the sight of another man residing over the table her dad used to sit at, or bumping into him on the landing. Nelly still lived in the house her parents had owned, and it would have been unbearable for her if Reggie had come to live with them. He had a lovely house of his own on the edge of the village and her mum seemed happy there, so the arrangement suited all three of them.

'It's Sunday – where do you think he is?' Jayne said with a fond smile.

'Golf?' Nelly hazarded a guess.

'You got it. Fancy a glass?' She picked up her wine. It was her mother's one indulgence – a glass of Pinot Grigio on a lazy weekend afternoon after the traditional roast had been consumed.

'I'd better not. If I start, I mightn't stop at one.' The way she was feeling, Nelly worried that she might just drink the whole bottle in one go.

'Tough week?' Jayne had half-shares in the business, and although she was for the most part a sleeping partner, she had a vested interest and she also did the accounts, so it wasn't unusual for the two of them to talk shop.

'You could say that,' Nelly sighed, as she sank into one of the squishy armchairs.

'Do you want to tell me about it?'

'I bumped into Isaac Richards.' Working with him could hardly be classed as "bumped" but it would do.

'Is he a new client?' Jayne was frowning.

'No, he's the architect at the stables on Muddypuddle Lane.'

'The cow shed conversion? What's he done? Or not done?' It wasn't unheard of for building contractors and architects to butt heads.

'Nothing – he's drawn up a decent set of plans. It's just...' Nelly took a deep breath. She had to get this off her chest or she might explode. 'I once knew him really well, Mum.'

Her mother's eyes widened. 'And seeing him again is a problem because...?'

'I was in love with him.'

'**When?** I haven't heard you mention him.' Her mother wore a shocked expression.

'In university.'

Jayne slowly closed her eyes and opened them again. 'I see. I knew you were upset, but I assumed it was because you dropped out of the course and because you were worried about your dad.'

'That was mostly it, but it wasn't the only reason.'

'I can see that now. Oh, love, I wish you'd stayed on to get your degree. Your dad and I begged you not to drop out.'

'And where would that have left him? He was worried sick about the business, and I wanted to take some of the burden.' Nelly couldn't have stayed in uni; her conscience wouldn't have allowed her.

'We'd have managed. You had your own life to lead, Nell. Neither me nor your father wanted you to sacrifice it for him.'

'I wanted to. I had to, Mum.'

Jayne's smile was soft and sad. 'You always were a daddy's girl. He couldn't take a step without you hot on his heels. He used to call you his little shadow.'

'I remember.'

'It used to scare me to death the way he took you onto building sites when you were small. I think you could hold a trowel before you could hold a crayon.'

'I loved every minute of it.' Nelly had tears in her eyes and she blinked them away.

'I wanted you to wear pretty dresses and curl your hair into ringlets, and you wanted to wear dungarees and have your hair in a ponytail to keep it out of the way.'

Nelly uttered a choked laugh. 'I still do.'

There was a pause for a while as they remembered the man who had played such a huge part in their lives, then her mum said, 'Do you still have feelings for this man?'

Nelly pulled a face. She didn't know what she was feeling, if she was honest. Confused didn't begin to explain it.

'Has seeing him again made you think about finishing your degree? Is that it?' her mum persisted.

'No, but even if I wanted to, it would be too late now.'

'It wouldn't,' Jayne insisted. 'You can do whatever you put your mind to.'

'What about Dad's business?'

'It's **your** business, and if you want to ask Gavin to manage it for you, or if you want to bring someone else in, or if you decide to sell it, that's up to you.'

Nelly supposed she **could** ask Gavin, her very capable and utterly loyal foreman, to run it for her, but she hesitated.

'I can't sell it.' She was adamant. Her dad had built the business from scratch, and over the years she'd fought fiercely to keep it going. She wasn't about to throw away all her hard work. Besides, she loved being in construction, she loved being her own boss, and she loved living in Picklewick.

'I'm sure the year and a half of the course that you've already done would count for something,' her mum was saying. 'So maybe you wouldn't have to repeat the whole thing?'

'I think I probably would, but I don't want to return to full-time education.'

Jayne was studying her shrewdly. 'If it's not giving up your degree that's got you all worked up, then it must be Isaac himself.'

When Nelly didn't say anything, her mum clambered out of her chair and put her arm around her shoulder. 'You didn't answer my question, but I don't think you need to. It's clear you **do** still have feelings for him. Did he love you?'

'I believe he did.'

'How does **he** feel about seeing you again?'

'No idea. Not much, I would have thought. It was a long time ago. He's moved on. So have I.'

Once again, her mum gave her a shrewd look. '**Have** you?'

Nelly couldn't answer her.

'Take my advice,' Jayne said, giving her a squeeze. 'Life is short. If you still care for him, do something about it.'

'He might be married or in a relationship.'

'If he is, then you walk away.'

'Even if he isn't, he mightn't feel the same way about me. It was such a long time ago,' Nelly repeated.

'If he doesn't, he doesn't. At least you'll know and can move on.'

Her mum's advice was sage, but Nelly wasn't convinced. It might be better to let sleeping dogs lie and not try to resurrect the past.

'You've been stagnating, Nell,' Jayne continued. 'I've often wondered why you haven't found love, and now I know. It's because you haven't been looking, have you?'

Her mum hit the nail on the head. Nelly **hadn't** been looking, and any boyfriends she'd had since Isaac had all been compared to him and found wanting. Her mum was wrong in one respect, though – Nelly **had** found love, but she'd walked away from it, and it had hurt so much that she wasn't sure she'd want to put herself through that ever again.

Anyway, Isaac no longer thought of her in that way. Whatever he'd felt about her in the past was long gone, so she'd only be making a fool of herself. Heck, he'd probably forgotten she existed and had only remembered when he'd seen her at the stables. Nothing he had done or said had given her any reason to think otherwise.

Nelly, she said to herself, **you're just going to have to get over it.**

But words were easy to say – doing it was a different matter entirely.

'I'll get these – what are you having?' Isaac's mate Frank leaned against the bar and eyed the pumps. 'They've got Stella on tap. You used to love a pint of Stella. Or six.'

Isaac chuckled. It was many years since he'd drunk lager, and even more years since he'd managed to sink more than a couple of pints. He must be getting old. 'A pint of Old Peculiar, please.' These days he preferred real ale, or wine, or even the occasional cocktail as long as it wasn't too sweet or fruity.

Frank caught the barman's attention and as he gave the man their drinks order, Isaac studied him. He hadn't seen Frank in years, not since he'd moved to Wiltshire.

He had met up with some of his other old school friends a couple of times since his return, but he hadn't done a great deal in the way of socialising, probably because nearly all of them had spouses or partners and several of them had children. Take Frank, for instance… Isaac hadn't seen him at all until this evening because he and his wife had four-month-old twins. Apparently, this was the first time he'd been out for ages, the poor bloke.

Even as he thought it, Isaac wasn't convinced there was anything "poor" about Frank. The man was glowing, despite the bags under his eyes, and the first thing he'd done when he'd spotted Isaac was to whip out his wallet and show him a photo of the babies.

Isaac felt a slap on his shoulder, and he turned around to see another old friend.

'Wotcha,' Chris said, easing his way between the two of them. For a Sunday evening the bar was crowded. 'She let you out then, Frank?' Chris teased. He turned to Isaac. 'His missus keeps a tight rein on him.'

Frank drew himself up to his full height. 'I'll have you know I like being at home. Do you realise I'm missing bath time to be out with you lot?'

'Yeah,' Chris conceded, 'I know what you mean, but you've got to let your hair down now and again, or the only thing you'll find yourself talking about is feeds and poo.'

'Poo?' Isaac raised his eyebrows.

'Believe me, it's a thing. When you've got kids, you become fascinated by the contents of their nappies.' Frank handed him his pint.

'Good grief!' Isaac took a deep draught, not wanting to think too closely about poo and nappies.

'I'd say you were lucky being single and kid-free, but I wouldn't mean it,' Chris said. 'I love my three to bits. Did I tell you that Levi is on the football team? He's only nine, but he's got a mean left kick on him. And Nenah is walking already and she's only ten months.'

The pride on Chris's face sent a bolt of envy right through Isaac and he bit his lip. It was strange seeing his old friends grown up and married, with kids of their own. The last time they'd had a proper get together, they'd still been kids themselves.

'Anyone on your horizon?' Frank asked him.

'Nah, as I said, he's single and fancy-free, aren't you, fella?' Chris gave him another slap on the back.

'Don't go telling my missis that – she'll be setting him up with one of her friends before you can say "mine's a pint".' Chris chuckled and raised his glass. 'Cheers.'

Isaac dutifully muttered 'Cheers,' and took a mouthful of the robust ale, wishing they'd change the subject. He didn't want to talk about his love life, or lack of it, and he definitely didn't want to talk about blind dates or being set up. He had enough to be going on with for the moment without romance.

Nelly's face flashed across his inner eye, and he shoved it away. Now was not the time to be thinking about lost love.

'What are you doing, workwise?' Frank asked a while later, after the conversation had moved on to football, cars and gaming, none of which Isaac was overly interested in. 'I hear you did the plans for that new house at the end of Trinity Street. They reckon it's going to be huge.'

'It will be fairly big,' Isaac said.

'And I've heard you did the plans for the cottages at the stables on Muddypuddle Lane,' Chris said.

'You heard right.'

'Nelly Newsome is doing the building work, isn't she?' Chris asked.

Frank said, 'She did the extension on my next-door neighbour's house. If we have any more kids, we might have to build one ourselves. We're bursting at the seams as it is. You could do the plans for us.'

'It would be my pleasure,' Isaac said. 'Just let me know when you're ready.'

'And I'd think about getting Nelly Newsome to build it,' Frank continued. 'Keep us posted and let us know how she gets on with those cottages. Tell me if you think she's any good.'

'She's good,' Isaac confirmed. He didn't want to discuss Nelly, but on the other hand he wanted to make sure people knew that her firm was one of the top ones in the area.

'Have you come across her before?'

'Once or twice,' Isaac admitted, but he didn't mean in a professional capacity.

'I'm not sure I'd want a woman building my extension,' Chris said, and Isaac inhaled sharply.

'You do realise that's extremely sexist,' he said. 'Anyway, I don't think she wields a hammer and chisel herself – she's got employees to do that for her. Although she **is** capable of building a house all by herself, if she wanted to.'

'You like her, don't you?' Chris was grinning.

'She's nice enough.'

'Look at him, he's gone all red.'

Isaac was aware of the heat in his face, and he took another swig of his pint to cover his embarrassment. 'I know her in a professional capacity,' he said, sounding incredibly pompous. 'I have no interest in her other than that.'

'Yeah, right,' Chris teased. 'I know a lost cause when I see one, and you look like you've got it bad.'

Isaac frowned. 'I'm not interested,' he repeated. 'I'm perfectly happy being single.' If he told himself that often enough maybe he'd believe it. Because at the moment he was consumed with envy and regret. Abruptly, Isaac realised he didn't want to be on his own, that he did want to be in a loving relationship. The problem was that the only woman he could imagine being in one with was

Nelly. Even after all this time and the way she'd dumped him, he still loved her, and in all those years no other woman had ever come close.

Petra gave Harry the gentlest of kisses on his nose. He stirred but didn't wake, so she crept out of the room as lightly as she could considering she was seven months pregnant, determined to check on the stables' newest arrival.

She felt absolutely shattered but she'd been unable to settle, not without checking on Star. Before she poked her head into the mare's stall, though, Petra couldn't resist taking a quick detour to have a look at the cow shed, so she grabbed a torch, crept out of the house and made her way down the track.

Flicking the torch on when she got to the cow shed, she shone the beam around the inside of the building and marvelled at how much had been achieved in such a small amount of time.

 The shed had been completely cleared and they'd even made a start on removing the ancient concrete base. The men had got to work with sledgehammers and crowbars, then Nathan had come in with the tractor and had levered most of the rest of it up, and carried the rubble off to be dumped in the pasture behind the cow shed, which was due to become a garden for the cottages and would now sport a rather large rockery. That had been Isaac's idea, and it would save them from having to try to get rid of the rubble. A rockery would be an ideal solution, and Lena had already offered to supply some plants from her own garden.

The generosity of people had taken Petra by surprise and she could feel her eyes welling up. Cross with herself, she blamed it on the pregnancy hormones. She wasn't usually such a cry baby, but lately she'd been bursting into tears at the drop of a hat.

She stood back, her hands on her hips, the darkness settling around her like a comforting blanket, and thought of how completely her life had changed over the past year. Not only was she soon to be a wife and a mother – which was mind-boggling in itself – but she was also about to expand the business in a way she never would have imagined.

Harry's vision of the cow shed becoming three cottages was inspired. She was still apprehensive about allowing him to sink his savings into the venture though; but apprehensive or not, it was too late to pull out now. The ball was well and truly in motion, so they had to see it through to the end.

Petra realised that some of her misgivings stemmed from a deep-rooted fear of something going wrong. What if things didn't work out in the long run between Harry and her? Where would that leave him? Or the stables?

Feeling rather foolish to be having such thoughts, especially considering they were about to get married and had a baby on the way, she gave herself a stern talking to. Nothing was going to go wrong. They had their whole lives ahead of them, and so much to be grateful for and to look forward to. It was just the baby hormones making her fretful.

Shaking her head at her silliness, she walked back to the stables and crossed the yard to the mare's stall. As soon as Amos had told her they were about to give a home to a pregnant mare in dire need of some TLC, Petra had moved Hercules out of his loosebox. It was the biggest and the one nearest the house, so she had given it to the mare for the duration, and that was where she was headed now.

The horse was skinnier than she should be and headshy. Petra guessed she'd been roughly treated, if not actually struck, and when she'd been led out of the horsebox, Petra's heart had gone out to her.

Her name was Star, on account of her having a white blob on her forehead, slightly off-centre. The rest of her was dark brown. Her coat ought to have been glossy with health, but it was dull and scruffy. She could do with a good grooming, but it would be a while before she had one; Petra wanted to let her settle in first and have her foal. There'd be time enough to make her pretty. Actually, she was quite pretty already, with a small head, neat ears, and a dish-shaped face. She was shy and nervous, but she'd allowed herself to be handled. Petra had almost sensed the relief in the animal when she'd been taken into a stall and the humans had retreated.

Star was indeed close to foaling, but a horse's gestation wasn't an exact science and she could give birth tonight, tomorrow, or tomorrow night. All Petra knew was that she wanted to be nearby when it happened to make sure everything went smoothly.

Quietly she opened the top door as unobtrusively as she could. The night lights around the yard threw some illumination, enough to make out the horse standing in the corner.

It also showed her something else – balancing on four ungainly legs was the most gorgeous little foal Petra had ever seen.

 And not only that, October was sitting on a sleeping bag on top of a pile of straw, and when she met Petra's astounded gaze she smiled, before her attention reverted back to the newest addition to the stables.

Petra stood there for a moment and studied the woman, a feeling of gratitude sweeping over her. She would never dream of asking anyone to spend the night in a stable with a vulnerable or sick horse – that was something she'd do herself – but Harry had made it clear that a night on a stable floor was no place for a pregnant woman, so she'd given in to his pleas to go to bed. But Petra knew she wouldn't be able to sleep until she'd checked on Star.

It looked like October must have had the same idea, but rather than leave the horse on her own, she'd decided to bunk down with her instead.

What an absolute gem she was!

Satisfied that Star was in good hands and that October would fetch her if anything was amiss, Petra whispered a soft, 'Thank you,' then quietly closed the top door and padded off.

Not quite ready to return to bed yet, she made a beeline for Hercules. The stallion was an ex-racehorse and was her pride and joy. Generally no one rode him but her, although that situation had changed since October had started working at the stables at the beginning of the year, because October was an extremely competent rider. With Petra being pregnant and unable to ride (she **was** able, but Harry had made her promise not to) someone had to exercise the horse.

'Hello, boy,' she murmured, and Hercules gave her a soft whicker in response and huffed out a sigh of greeting.

He wandered over to the stable door and hung his head over it, allowing her to scratch his nose and tickle him under the chin. He suffered the attention for a short while, then he jerked his head up and retreated into his stall.

'I know, time for bed, right?' With a final pat on his haunches Petra left Hercules in peace and went for a stroll around the rest of the yard and the outbuildings.

May was one of her favourite months and in the stillness of the night air she could smell the honeysuckle that had draped itself over the fence, and the sound of lambs bleating for their mothers carried from the hillside opposite.

She could hear the chickens moving restlessly in their coop, and she called out softly to let them know that it was their friendly human corn-giver outside, and not a predatory fox. She would have liked to have a quick look at the chicks, but they were safely tucked up for the night and she didn't want to disturb them. She'd quickly check on Princess though, because she was another creature at the stables that was about to give birth any day, and Petra was looking forward to having a kid around. Baby goats were so funny and inquisitive, and so full of the joys of life.

When she crept into the barn expecting to see the goat asleep, Princess also had a surprise for her. Curled in the straw at her feet lay a tiny baby, the mother standing guard over the new arrival.

'Oh, aren't you clever!' Petra exclaimed, pulling the moveable fence to one side so she could slip through and take a closer look at the kid.

Princess eyed her warily, but she allowed Petra to pick the little creature up and check it over.

'You've got a little girl,' she said to her, 'and she's perfect.' The tiny baby smelled of the straw she'd been lying in, milk, and a not-unpleasant goaty scent. And she was so soft and cuddly, despite being over 50 per cent knobbly, wobbly legs.

Petra put her down and the kid immediately staggered over to her mother and searched for a teat, her little tail waggling furiously when she found it. Princess made a low grumbling sound in her throat that Petra knew was contentment, so she left the pair alone to continue to bond.

As she retraced her steps, she paused for a moment, seeing quick scudding movements in the field beyond. Rabbits! Loads of them, lolloping and hopping around, and amongst the tufts of grass she could see baby rabbits darting to and fro. It made her heart sing to see them.

As if sensing her joy, the baby kicked inside her, and Petra's hands automatically went to her stomach. 'It'll be your turn before you know it,' she whispered, but even that small noise was picked up by the rabbits, and en masse they scurried for cover.

'You've scared them off,' she said to her son. 'Never mind, as soon as we've gone, they'll come back out again. I can't wait for you to see them. Although, by the time you put in an appearance, they'll be nearly full grown.' She continued to stroke her tummy, convinced that her baby could hear and understand every word she said, but eventually she began to feel tired.

Satisfied that everything was as it should be, and feeling incredibly content and lucky, Petra returned to her bed and the arms of her husband-to-be.

CHAPTER FIVE

Nelly breathed deeply, got a noseful of horse aroma, and coughed, lamenting her stupidity. She'd lived in and around Picklewick for long enough to know that fresh air, when it came to rural locations, wasn't always as fresh as one hoped.

She took another hesitant breath, and a gust of wind brought the more appealing scent of the ferns on the hillside above and the crab apple blossom in the hedgerows. A faint hint of sheep was also in the air, adding to the mix of smells.

As she strolled across the yard, she spied Petra shooing several brown hens out of a stable, and she made her way over to her.

'Hi,' she called. 'How did the clearing go? Sorry I had to dash off,' she added as she grew closer. The chickens darted past, and Nelly froze, worried she might step on one of them or they might peck her. She tended to prefer her chicken on a plate in a sauce, rather than strutting around her feet.

'The blasted things get everywhere,' Petra grumbled. 'I was just about to jab my pitchfork into the straw when three of them fluttered out and gave me the fright of my life. Why don't you take a look for yourself?'

Without waiting for an answer, Petra walked away, leaving Nelly no option other than to follow her. Thankfully, she hadn't seen Isaac's car in the stables' car park, so she was as certain as she could be that he wasn't on site. However, she didn't fully relax until she rounded the corner of the shed and could see inside.

Harry and Nathan were there, but they were on their own, she noticed with relief. She was also pleased to see how much work had been accomplished in just twenty-four hours. The shed was empty, and the concrete floor had been removed and dug down to a depth of about a metre. Harry and Nathan were in the middle of clearing away the last of the rubble.

'That's great,' she said. 'I was hoping my men could get started soon. They're just finishing up a job and should be here on Wednesday, if that's all right with you?'

Petra nodded. 'Definitely! The sooner you start, the sooner you'll finish. Ideally, I'd like most of the work done by the time this one puts in an appearance.' She rubbed her tummy.

Nelly pulled a face. 'Two months is a bit optimistic,' she warned. 'I've prepared a schedule of works that I can email over to you, if you'd like to have a look at it. But I warn you, there is some flexibility built into it – very few jobs run to plan. I reckon, assuming all the subcontractors stick to the schedule that it will take five months from start to completion.'

'That long?' Petra sounded dismayed.

'I did tell Harry this,' Nelly said, and winced when Petra shot Harry a cross look.

Oh dear, Nelly thought, hoping that this wasn't an indication of the way things were going to be on this build. That was the problem when clients didn't employ a project manager, and wanted to do it themselves, and it was even more of an issue when the clients failed to discuss things with each other. Luckily, Nelly was fully capable of managing the project, if only they'd let her get on with it.

'Have you ordered the windows yet?' Nelly asked, trying to draw Petra's attention away from her hapless fiancé.

'Not yet. Should I have done?'

'Sooner is better than later,' Nelly advised. 'Isaac hasn't planned for anything out of the ordinary, but I'd still get the ball rolling if I were you. Some companies can take a while to manufacture them.'

'I think I do need that schedule of works,' Petra said, with a frown.

Nelly took pity on her. 'The schedule is for me and my men to refer to, but what if I add in all the things you need to be doing, and when you need to do them? Would that help?' So much for her rule of not doing more than she was contracted to do, Nelly thought with a sigh.

'That would be marvellous! Thank you. Although I don't know when I'm going to find the time to go shopping for windows.'

'You'll have to, if you want this project completed,' Nelly warned. There wasn't any point in beating around the bush, and she wasn't afraid of telling her clients the truth, no matter how much they didn't want to hear it.

'I suppose.' Petra made a face. 'You must think I'm a right pain in the arse.'

'Not at all. You're just inexperienced in this kind of stuff.' Taking pity on her once again, Nelly added, 'Pick the materials you want to use for the frames, pick the patterned glass you'll need for the bathroom windows, and pick the style of door and window handles, then give them a copy of the plans and let the company work from those. It shouldn't take more than a couple of hours to get them ordered. But don't pay more than a 20 per cent deposit until the windows are in and you're happy with them.'

'Thanks, that's a great help. Now all I've got to do is to decide on the boilers, the radiators, the flooring, the bathrooms, the kitchens...' Petra trailed off.

Nelly stared at her for a second, then the two of them burst out laughing at the same time.

Harry wandered over, dusting his hands off against the backside of his jeans. 'Glad to see you're having fun while me and Nathan are working our socks off,' he teased, giving Petra a kiss on the cheek. 'Come to check on us?' This was directed at Nelly.

'Yep. I want to know when I can send my men in. I told Petra Wednesday, if that's okay with everyone?' Nelly wasn't sure who she was supposed to be reporting to – Petra, Harry, Amos, or all three of them.

'Wednesday is fine,' Harry said, as Nathan, who'd finished scooping up the final load of concrete, joined them. 'I've been thinking that it might be a good idea to get some hardcore and chippings delivered to put on the track leading to the cowshed. I expect you'll have some trucks and lorries going up and down, and I'm worried the surface won't be able to cope with it.' He looked at Nathan for confirmation, and Nathan nodded. 'We'll need to tarmac it eventually, but I didn't want to do it just yet.'

'Good thinking,' Nelly said. 'There'll be a caravan here tomorrow, and that's only the start of it.'

'A caravan? You don't live in it, do you?' Petra looked shocked and Nelly hastened to reassure her.

'Not at all. No one lives in it, but there's a loo inside and cooking facilities, so the guys can take their breaks in comfort.'

'Wow, I didn't expect that,' Harry said.

'Neither did they! I used to arrange for a portaloo and they ate their sandwiches sitting in the van if it was wet, as did I. But I hated it, and as I'm on site almost as much as they are, I came up with the idea of a caravan. It's more comfortable and in the long run it's worked out cheaper than hiring a portaloo,' she added.

Nathan gave Petra a meaningful look.

'Don't start getting any ideas,' Petra warned. 'You can come into the house whenever you want.'

'I wouldn't mind a caravan down on the bottom field,' he joked, and Petra rolled her eyes.

'Now look what you've started,' she complained to Nelly.

Nelly grinned. This was one of the reasons why her workmen were so loyal – because she looked after them. Her dad always used to say that one good worker was worth three average ones, and she'd built her business's reputation by being able to attract and hang on to the best brickies, plasterers, general labourers, and roofers for miles around. Not all of them worked exclusively for her, but because she was fair with them, the ones who weren't on the books were always happy to help her out if she had a rush job on.

She was about to leave, when Petra said, 'Would you like to see a baby goat? She was only born last night and she's so damned cute.'

How could Nelly resist? 'Yes, please!'

'Follow me.' Petra began walking up the track, Nelly falling into step alongside her.

'We had a mare give birth last night too, but I'm trying to keep her as quiet as possible so I won't show you the foal today.'

When Petra went on to explain how badly Star had been treated, Nelly was appalled. 'Thank goodness you were on hand to take her in,' she said, glad that she'd gone the extra mile to help Petra out. Good people like her, Harry and Amos deserved all the help they could get.

'Oh, my goodness! Look how cute that is!' Nelly exclaimed when she saw the little kid. 'I want one! I've got nowhere to keep it, and no idea how to look after it, but I want one.'

'You won't when you see what they grow into,' Petra laughed. 'Princess, her mum, is a nightmare. She's an escape artist, and she eats anything she can get hold of.'

Nelly spent a few minutes gazing at the little animal, then she said goodbye to Petra and made her way into Picklewick. It was coming up for lunchtime, so she thought she'd pop into the village and pick up a sandwich before she went to the job her men were currently finishing.

As she drove down the lane, her thoughts refused to stay on work: they kept straying towards Isaac and the chat she'd had with her mum. Did she have the courage to take her mum's advice, or should she hunker down and try to pretend she didn't still have feelings for him?

One thing she did know – she fervently wished he hadn't come back into her life, because she had been doing just fine.

Now though, she wondered whether she'd ever be fine again.

'I'm going to have to get off in a minute,' Harry said to Nathan after Nathan had taken the last load of earth and stones that had been lying under the concrete base of the cow shed and dumped it on what was shortly going to become a rockery. It didn't look particularly attractive at the moment, but Harry had every faith in Amos's green fingers. 'Will you be okay sorting out the water and the electrics? I've got a couple of ponies to shoe,' he added.

Harry and Nathan had planned to hook up a previously disused tap that had supplied mains water to the shed in the past, and run an extension cable from the barn. The shed did have its own electricity supply, but it was old and would need rewiring.

'I can manage,' Nathan assured him.

'I want to thank you for all your help this weekend. I know it's not in your job description.'

Nathan chortled. 'You do know I haven't got a job description? Megan keeps teasing me about that. Seriously, I'm happy to help.'

Harry was touched. In the year since he'd known Nathan, they'd become friends and he knew that both Petra and Amos regarded him as a member of the family, rather than an employee.

'Can you do me a favour?' he asked.

'Anything,' Nathan said, without hesitation.

'Can you keep an eye on Petra when I'm not around? I know she's anxious about trying to get as much done as possible before the baby comes, and I'm worried about her overdoing it.'

Nathan looked affronted. 'You don't need to ask. I'm doing that anyway.'

'Good – between us maybe we can get her to slow down. Guess what she was doing last night when she should have been in bed?'

'Checking on Star. I know, October told me.'

'I know October spent the night in Star's stable. Did the pair of you cook that up between you?'

Nathan grinned. 'We did. It was supposed to be my turn tonight if the mare hadn't had her foal by then. I'm gutted I missed it.'

'Yeah, so's Petra,' Harry chuckled. 'She thought she'd got away with sneaking out, but she made the mistake of putting her cold feet on me when she came back to bed. See what I mean about her overdoing it?'

'You'll not change her,' Nathan warned. 'She's as stubborn as Princess and just as cantankerous.'

'Tell me about it!' was Harry's heartfelt reply. Then he softened. 'I wouldn't want to. She's perfect as she is.'

Nathan clapped him on the shoulder. 'Not as perfect as my Megan.'

'I think we'll have to agree to disagree,' Harry joked. 'Seriously, let me know if you think she's doing too much. I can scale back my farrier commitments and help around the stables more. I'm planning on doing that anyway, once the baby arrives. I can't wait! And neither can Petra but for a different reason – I don't think she's too keen on being pregnant. She's complaining of backache, being unable to sleep, the baby using her as a punching bag, Braxton Hicks...'

'Who is he?'

Harry stared at Nathan for a second, before he understood what he was asking. 'Braxton Hicks are what they call it when the uterus contracts and relaxes. It's a kind of practice for labour.'

'I see.' Nathan grimaced.

'Sorry, mate. You don't need to hear all this. But if you see her wince and rub her stomach, she's either being pummelled from the inside out, or she's—'

'I get the picture,' Nathan said hurriedly. 'Please don't tell me anything else.'

Harry laughed. 'Yet you'd have happily stayed with Star when she foaled.'

'That's different.' Nathan lifted his chin and refused to look at him. 'Star isn't my boss.'

'That horse was having a good go at bossing you around when you fed her this morning,' Harry pointed out. 'I saw her trying to stick her nose in your pocket, looking for a treat. She's only been here five minutes and she's got you wrapped around her hoof.'

'I feel sorry for her,' Nathan said. 'She deserves a bit of love and attention.'

'She certainly does. I have to confess to trying to give her a handful of pony nuts earlier, but she wouldn't come anywhere near me.'

'You've either got it, or you haven't,' Nathan replied with a smirk. 'She'll take a while to trust people again, but she'll get there. She's settled in well and she's got her baby to keep her occupied.' He paused. 'Don't worry about Petra – I'll do my best to keep her out of mischief. It'll be hard, mind you, because she's never been one to sit down and put her feet up, and the nearer it gets to your baby's arrival the more nesty she's becoming. She's like a bitch about to whelp. I'll be expecting her to make a den under the stairs soon.'

'I've noticed that – Amos caught her cleaning the boot room the other day. He had to threaten her with no supper if she didn't behave herself. No wonder she says she's exhausted.' Harry sighed. Pregnancy was a whole new experience for the two of them, but as he'd said to her the other night, they'd know more when they had the next one.

He'd had to duck when she threw Queenie's chew at him.

Isaac's head was swimming with ideas as he strode away from what he was hoping would be his next client.

The house was in Picklewick and the ladies who owned it wanted an extension leading out from the kitchen, and the whole of the downstairs turned into one large, airy space, with open plan kitchen, dining and living areas. In addition, there would be an attic conversion and a roof terrace above the new extension, with skylights. But what they wanted was something unusual – the "wow" factor – and it was down to him to deliver it.

He was intending to return to his office to sketch out a few options to show them, but first he wanted some lunch, so he decided to take a walk down Picklewick's high street and pop into a café. If he ate a substantial meal now, he could work into the evening without his stomach protesting too much.

It was while he was strolling along, wondering which of the two cafes he wanted to eat in, that he spotted Nelly. He'd been glancing in through the window of the first one he'd come to, and when he took a step towards the entrance, she was right there in front of him.

He came to a sudden halt, his heart
hammering.

It was silly of him not to anticipate seeing
her here. After all, this was where she
lived, he was on her turf, in her neck of
the woods. Half of him wondered if that
was what had driven him to walk down
the high street in the first place. He could
so easily have chosen somewhere near
the office. There had been absolutely no
need for him to come into Picklewick, but
he had done so anyway, and it occurred
to him that his subconscious knew more
about what he wanted than he did.

Nelly was staring at him, her eyes wide,
her lips set in a line. He wondered what
she was thinking. She didn't seem
pleased to see him at all.

'Hi,' he said uncertainly.

She shrugged. 'Hi.'

'What are you doing here?' he asked, then immediately realised it was a stupid question.

'I live here. What's your excuse?'

'I've just been to see a client – a big extension, attic conversion...' He trailed off.

She studied him for a moment. 'I've been to the stables on Muddypuddle Lane. They've done most of the clearing. In fact, they've probably done it all by now. I told them I'll start work on Wednesday. Is that okay with you?'

'Of course it is. I've done my bit, it's all down to you now. I'm here if you need me, though.'

'Glad to hear it.'

From her tone he realised that she'd probably had issues with architects in the past. He knew it happened occasionally, especially when clients changed their minds halfway through a build and wanted additional features, or something removed. Sometimes, if the change was substantial enough, it might even mean a re-submission to the planning department, which could hold up a build indefinitely.

Suddenly, and without any conscious decision on his part, he found himself saying, 'I was just about to grab some lunch. Would you care to join me?'

He could almost see the cogs whirring in her brain as she considered his suggestion.

Okay,' she agreed slowly. 'That's what I came into the village to do anyway.' She sounded incredibly reluctant and he almost wished he hadn't asked her, but he had done and she'd agreed, so he couldn't go back on it now.

'Will this do?' He glanced at the cafe, and when she nodded, he held his arm out, inviting her to go ahead of him.

Following her inside, he couldn't help studying her. She still had the most incredible figure and he was so intent on watching the sway of her hips as she walked in front of him, that he almost bumped into her when she stopped.

'If you tell me what you want,' he said, 'I'll order and you can grab a table.'

'I'll order for myself, thank you.' She sounded prickly and defensive, and he wondered what he had said to upset her. Then he got it — she didn't want to feel indebted to him. She wanted to pay her own way.

'Okay,' he acquiesced airily, not wanting to make a big deal out of it. It was only a sandwich and a coffee, for goodness sake. 'You go first.'

Nelly narrowed her eyes at him, then ordered, and when she'd finished she found a table and sat down. He quickly joined her and as they waited for their lunches to arrive, he scrabbled around for something to say. Work seemed to be the safest option, so he started with that.

'Have you got another job on at the moment?' he asked.

She leaned back in her seat and folded her hands on the table. 'Two, although one of them will be done by tomorrow, except for the snagging.'

He nodded. Snagging made the difference between a customer being delighted with a job or complaining for weeks. He suspected that any issues at the end of one of Nelly's builds would only be minor and easily solvable.

'Which is why I can pull most of them off this job and get them started up at the stables,' she continued.

'Did you know Petra or Harry before this?' he asked.

'Not really. I knew of the stables, and I've seen Petra and Amos around, but I didn't much care for horses or riding, so the first time I went there was when they asked me to give them a quote. Harry is new to the village – or newish; he's been here about a year, I think.'

'They seem like nice people,' Isaac said.

'They are.'

An awkward silence descended, and Isaac's heart constricted. He was finding it hard to believe that the woman he'd once known so intimately and who he'd been able to share his innermost thoughts with, was now a total stranger. But then again, what had he expected? Nelly had become a stranger the second she'd dumped him, so perhaps he hadn't known her as well as he thought he had.

He glanced at her, caught her eye, and looked away, but when he looked back she was still gazing at him. Was there a softness in her that hadn't been there a minute ago, or was he imagining it?

'Is it strange being back?' she asked, and he took a moment to answer.

'Yes and no. In some respects, I feel as though I've never been away.' He thought back to last night – some of the banter he'd shared with his friends had been remarkably similar to the rubbish they'd spouted when they were teenagers. 'But in others, things are very different. I've got my own place for a start, and I run my own business. And everyone has changed around me. In my head they should still be the same age as when I last saw them, and places should still look the same. Did you know that the old cinema has closed down and they've built a multi-screen one?'

'I did know – it's near the supermarket.'

He shook his head, partly in wonderment and partly in despair. 'It feels weird,' he admitted. 'Picklewick hasn't changed much though.' He'd only visited the village a couple of times in his youth, despite it being just nine or so miles away from his hometown.

'That's both a blessing and a curse,' Nelly said. Abruptly, she looked beyond him, over his shoulder towards the door, and a smile transformed her face.

Isaac twisted in his seat, wondering who it was that she was so pleased to see, and wishing she'd smile at him like that. To his dismay, he saw William – the guy who managed Picklewick's care home – and his heart sank.

His instincts had been right, after all. She'd gone to the stables on Saturday because William had been there, and not to see how things were going with the clearing party or to have a beer and a burger, and certainly not because she'd thought Isaac might be there. She'd been all dressed up for William.

Blast, the man was coming over, and his focus was on Nelly.

Isaac squirmed uncomfortably as William asked, 'May I?' and pointed to an empty chair.

'Of course,' Nelly said.

Isaac wanted to tell him to get lost, but instead he smiled and nodded a greeting, dismay flooding through him. At least her interest in this guy might explain why she'd dashed off on Saturday. She clearly hadn't wanted to be alone with **him**, however briefly.

Suddenly Isaac couldn't face sitting there with the two lovebirds, and he leapt to his feet. 'Sorry, I've just remembered something,' he garbled, and he whirled on his heel and shot out of the door, leaving a bemused server staring after him.

As he hurried to his car, he wrestled with the knowledge that he'd probably made the wrong decision in returning to the area. He might live several miles away from Picklewick, but it was inevitable he and Nelly would continue to bump into each other.

But he couldn't consider relocating again – not when his mum needed him and his business was just becoming established. Workwise there would be a long way to go before he was in the same position as he had been in Wiltshire, but he was getting there.

So he was stuck here, whether he liked it or not, and he rued his rash decision to move nearer to his mum. Why couldn't he have simply visited her every weekend until she was back on her feet?

Yeah, and when would that be, he asked himself? It had already been seven months since his mum and dad had split up, and she was only marginally better now than she had been when it had first happened. If Isaac didn't know better, he would have thought his dad had died, not walked out.

But then, hadn't he felt the same way himself when Nelly had walked out of his life? So he could understand how his mum was feeling. He'd been in a dark place for months too, and his and Nelly's relationship had only lasted for a fraction of the time that his mum and dad had been married. No wonder it was taking her ages to get over it, and he was beginning to fear she never would.

Gah, he was sorely tempted to give his dad a piece of his mind, and he would have done so if he thought it would do any good. Funnily enough though, he didn't get the feeling that his father had left his mum because of another woman. The place his dad was renting was devoid of any feminine touches whatsoever, Isaac had observed during the twice he'd been there, so he wondered if it was an affair that had split his parents up (and the other woman was no longer on the scene) or whether it was because of something else entirely.

Sighing to himself as he drove out of Picklewick and made his way back to his office, Isaac was aware that he'd made his bed and he had to lie in it. Nelly had moved on with her life – he hadn't expected anything less. As far as he'd been concerned, she'd moved on the minute she'd told him she was dropping out of the course and going home. So, in effect, nothing had changed as far as that situation went.

But what **had** changed was the realisation that he still felt the same way about her as he'd felt all those years ago. He still loved her, and there wasn't a damned thing he could do about it.

What the hell was wrong with the man? Nelly asked herself as she watched Isaac dash out of the café and stomp up the road.

Was it something she'd said, or not said? Had he taken a dislike to William? Though how he could do such a thing was beyond her. As far as she knew, the two men had only met on Saturday, and William was such a lovely guy she didn't know how anyone could possibly dislike him.

Which brought her full circle to thinking that it must be because of her. Her mum's advice to do something about it if she still loved him was all well and good, because she **had** done something about it – she'd agreed to have lunch with him – and look where that had got her.

Oh, well, at least she knew where she stood; he'd made it clear he wasn't interested in her. But the other part of her mum's advice (to move on) simply wasn't going to happen, either.

Nelly hadn't imagined ever seeing Isaac again after she'd dumped him, therefore she'd had thirteen years in which to move on. But she hadn't done so, because she'd never stopped loving him. And if she hadn't found love again in all that time, she was unlikely to find it now.

'Is everything all right?' William asked.

Nelly jerked herself out of her thoughts. 'Eh?'

'You were miles away.' He was looking at her with concern.

'Yes, sorry, everything's fine.'

Poor William, despite him sitting right next to her, she'd forgotten he was there. She'd been so focused on Isaac and the way he'd walked out without any warning, that William had faded into the background.

He must think her really rude – and goodness knows what he must think of Isaac. He'd only just sat down when...

Nelly froze as a thought struck her.

Isaac hadn't left because he had suddenly remembered that he had to be somewhere or do something. That hadn't been a "damn it, I've forgotten something" expression on his face. Isaac had been **upset**. She'd known his every expression, his every gesture, so intimately – **something** had upset him.

One minute he'd been sitting there, chatting – okay, it might have been a little awkward, but that was to be expected considering they were just getting to know one another again, plus there was the elephant in the room of the way things had ended between them – and the next, he'd jumped to his feet and dashed off.

As far as Nelly could see the only thing to have changed was William's arrival, and as she'd already considered and dismissed the possibility that Isaac might have taken a dislike to inoffensive, kind, considerate William, she was left with another scenario.

Had Isaac shot off because he was under the impression that she and William were an item?

Surely not? William was—

'Here you go, love,' the waitress said, putting two plates of sandwiches on the table. She turned to William. 'Your toastie will just be a tick. Is the other gentleman coming back?' Curiosity filled her face.

'I don't think so, but leave them here anyway,' Nelly said.

William was gazing quizzically at her. 'He didn't say where he was going, did he? I could always ask for them to be wrapped up and I could pop them into him on the way to work.'

'That's kind of you,' she said, 'but I don't think you need to bother. He'll be miles away by now.'

See, William **was** a nice guy. A very nice guy. But even so, Isaac had nothing to worry about in that regard. If, in fact, he was worried at all. Which he probably wasn't.

Flipping heck! She wished she knew what Isaac was thinking, but she had no intention of making a fool of herself by asking him.

CHAPTER SIX

Even for the beginning of June, the weather was unseasonably warm and Isaac felt a trickle of sweat run down his back as he walked across the yard, heading for the former cow shed. He called it "former" because in the space of a couple of weeks it had been transformed. Nelly and her team were doing a fantastic job.

Not that he'd seen much of her – he'd managed to miss her so far whenever he'd paid the site a visit. The avoidance was deliberate on his part.

But today her van was here, and he wondered whether the heat he was suddenly feeling had more to do with seeing her again than the temperature. He'd not set eyes on her since the café incident a couple of weeks ago, and that was the way he wanted it to stay. But it was unrealistic of him to think he could avoid her forever, and if he drove off now, someone was bound to notice and wonder what the problem was. The last thing he wanted was for people to speculate, or for his clients to think there was something wrong. Therefore, he straightened his shoulders, lifted his chin, and prepared himself to meet his nemesis once more.

'Back again?' Gavin joked as he rounded the corner. 'I've never known such a hands-on architect.'

Isaac shrugged. 'I like to make sure my plans are being followed,' he said, then wished he hadn't as he saw Gavin prickle at the unmeant insinuation that Isaac didn't trust the builders to do a good job.

'Oi, Nell! This man is saying we can't follow a set of drawings,' Gavin called, and Isaac winced.

Nelly was standing in the open doorway of the caravan that Nelly had put on the site for the comfort of her workforce.

'I didn't—' he began, then he noticed Gavin smirking and he realised he'd been set up. Maybe he hadn't disguised his feelings for her as well as he'd hoped.

'Tea?' Her voice was curt, but at least she was speaking to him.

Without waiting for an answer, Nelly went inside the caravan and, after a brief hesitation during which he wondered whether it was such a good idea to get so close to her knowing how he still felt, he followed her inside.

To his surprise the interior of the van was as clean as a new pin, and his astonishment must have registered on his face because Nelly said, 'If they don't keep it clean and tidy, they don't get to use it on the next job. I'm not their nursemaid and I'm not cleaning up after them.'

She didn't say anything further about it, but he guessed that in the early days one or two of her men might have been under the impression that because Nelly was a woman, it might be down to her to keep the place clean. Isaac would have loved to have been a fly on the wall when that particular issue was aired. He bet she would have put them in their place in no uncertain terms.

Abruptly he wondered just how hard it must have been for her – a female in a predominantly masculine world. In the beginning her dad would have still been on the scene in the background to give her guidance and advice, but after Ken had passed, Isaac couldn't begin to imagine what her life must have been like. In her early twenties and trying to run a construction business... it must have been tough.

Nelly handed him a mug of dark brown liquid. 'Sorry, I make builder's tea as a force of habit. Would you like more milk?'

'It's fine.' He didn't care how strong the tea was – his focus was on Nelly. He placed the mug on the side without tasting its contents. 'You're doing sterling work on the shed,' he said.

Her lips twitched. 'I thought you were worried about my men's ability to follow plans?'

'Nope, not me. I have every faith in you.'

'Pleased to hear it.'

'I always did have.'

Nelly looked down, her gaze on the mug she held. 'I didn't,' she replied quietly.

'It must have been hard.'

'It was.'

'And now?'

'Only when a client expects a fifty-something bloke to turn up, and he or she gets me.'

'Are the men worse or the women?'

'It's an even split.' She looked up at him. 'But let's not talk about gender bias in the workplace.'

'Okay. What **do** you want to talk about?'

Her eyebrows rose and she tilted her head to the side. 'The build, of course.'

'Of course.' Isaac didn't know what he'd been hoping for – her telling him that she and William were no longer an item, maybe? He said, 'It appears to be ahead of schedule.'

'It is. I'm hoping to have it watertight by the end of July.'

'You won't need me after that, unless there's a problem,' he observed.

'I don't need you now.'

'Right...' That put him in his place. It was hardly surprising that he wasn't needed. This job wasn't particularly technical, or large. It was a straightforward barn conversion that required a decent set of technical drawings (which he'd supplied) so any further consultation with the architect would usually only take place if something was unclear, or the build hit an unforeseen problem. Yet, here he was, still buzzing around and as welcome as a wasp at a picnic.

Nelly barked out a laugh. 'That came out wrong. I only meant that your drawings are good. Excellent, in fact.'

'Thanks.' His reply was dry. He sipped his virtually undrinkable tea and hunted around for something to say.

She beat him to it. 'You left in a hurry the other day. Was there a problem?'

Yeah, your boyfriend, he nearly said. 'Er, my mum. I suddenly remembered I said I'd call in to see her before my next appointment. Sorry.'

Nelly shrugged. 'These things happen. How is she?'

'Mum and Dad split up last year and she hasn't coped with it too well. That's the reason I came back here to live.'

'I'm sorry to hear that. How are you feeling about it?'

Isaac blinked. Nelly was the first person to ask how **he** felt. Everyone else had been (quite rightly) more concerned with how his mum was coping. But Isaac was hurting, too. Although he was still in contact with his father, the parental home that he thought was a permanent and steadfast feature in his life, was in tatters. Never in a million years would he have imagined that they would split up. Their love had been so strong, so sure... Isaac simply couldn't think what had gone wrong.

'I'm okay,' he replied, slowly.

Nelly scrutinised him. 'I don't believe you are.'

Isaac paused. They had known each other inside-out once, to the extent that they'd been able to tell what the other was thinking. Until one day she'd told him they were over, and he realised that he hadn't known what she was thinking at all.

Obviously it hadn't happened as abruptly or as cleanly as that. When Nelly's mum had shared the news that her dad was unwell, no one realised the extent of his illness. Nelly had travelled back and forth between uni and home for a while, struggling to keep up with the course, Isaac doing all he could to help, both of them believing it was only for the short term.

Then one day Nelly had slipped into his room in the house he shared with three other students, her eyes red, her expression anguished, and he'd held her as she cried.

He'd continued to hold her until she'd told him it was over between them, that she was dropping out of uni and going back home to live for the rest of the academic year.

Even then, he hadn't truly believed that had been the end of their relationship, of their love. He fully expected her to return to university, to resume the second year of her course and for the two of them to pick up where they'd left off.

It hadn't happened. Nelly had left for good and cut off all contact with him.

It had broken his heart. And now here she was, thinking she knew him, thinking she knew how he was feeling...

How dare she!

'You don't know me,' he said, his voice quiet, his temper rising.

Nelly flushed and looked away. 'I deserved that.'

Isaac didn't respond.

'I'm sorry if I hurt you,' she continued, a hitch in her voice.

'There is no **if** about it.'

Was she really going to do this now? Did he want to do this at all? Briefly he debated walking away: after all, she'd already told him that his presence on site wasn't needed. **But**, they were living in roughly the same area – him in town, her here in Picklewick – and they would unquestionably meet again, if not on this job, then on another. It was better they cleared the air now, so if they had to work together in the future they could do so as old friends rather than former lovers.

Yeah, right... his heart said – as if **that** was going to happen, not when he still felt the same way about her as he had all those years ago. He had no intention of letting her know that, of course. So he stayed, and prayed he could walk out of the caravan with his pride intact. It was far too late to hope his heart would be – that particular part of him had been shattered a long time ago. Even now he could feel the jagged shards of it grinding together. Damn – would this pain **never** go away? It had been thirteen flipping years!

'It hurt me just as much,' she said.

Isaac's laugh was harsh and bitter. 'Really?'

Nelly's eyes suddenly filled with tears, and he relented. He had to remember that she'd felt she had no choice, and her father had passed away, presumably as a result of the illness that had driven Nelly to leave university, the course, and him. Maybe she'd felt she hadn't had any choice, but – damn it! – she should have spoken to him about it. They could have worked something out.

'Sorry,' he said. 'You must have had your reasons.' Yeah, the reason was that she hadn't loved him enough to try to make it work. She hadn't loved him as much as he'd loved her.

'Do you want to hear them?' she asked.

'Bit late, isn't it? Thirteen years too late.'

'I didn't expect to ever see you again.'

'And now that you have, you feel the need to unburden yourself? Are you feeling guilty by any chance?'

Nelly got to her feet. 'Sorry, this is a bad idea. I'm going now. I need to check how

they're getting on with the roof joists.'
She brushed past him, heading for the
door.

The scent of her invaded his nose and his
heart constricted in pain.

Without thinking, Isaac grabbed hold of
her arm, bringing her up short, and she let
out a squeak.

Mortified, he released her. 'Sorry, I had no
right to do that.'

Nelly's gaze bored into him. 'No, you
didn't.'

'Did I hurt you?'

Mutely, she shook her head, but her hand
went to her arm and she rubbed the area
where his fingers had been. He hadn't
intended to touch her, and the shock of it
reverberated through his whole body.

She hadn't moved, and her face was so close to his that he could feel her breath on his lips. Her eyes were huge and luminous, her pupils dark depths that a man could lose his soul in.

Isaac had already lost his to her. He'd lost it thirteen years ago...

With an anguished groan he gathered her to him. His lips found hers and they staggered back until she was up against the door, then he was kissing her with a passion he'd forgotten he'd possessed. Nelly kissed him back, her body moulding against him, an intoxicating blend of the familiar and the new. Her mouth opened, inviting him in, and his tongue found hers, to tease and tantalise.

Her whimper of desire struck him deep in the solar plexus and his arousal, immediate and intense, threatened to sweep him away with the force of his desire. He wanted her so badly that his very soul ached with longing.

Nelly squirmed against him, pressing herself into him, and he panted against her lips as he struggled to maintain control of himself.

He was going to claim her, here, now, against the door, and with her answering breathy sigh, he knew she was as eager for this as he.

His hand slid down her back, cupping her buttock and—

The door to the caravan rattled and he froze. So did Nelly.

'Hello? Nelly? Are you in there?' a man's voice called.

Isaac dragged his mouth from hers and Nelly pushed him away. He took a step back as she darted around him to stand in the middle of the caravan's tiny living space, her expression stricken.

Abruptly, Isaac came to his senses. What was he doing? What were **they** doing?

Her eyes were dark with passion, her cheeks flushed with desire, and her lips swollen from his kisses. Never had she looked so beautiful, and never had he desired her as much as he did right then. But that way madness lay, and heartache, and she'd already caused him enough of that for one lifetime.

'I'm sorry,' he muttered, his voice hoarse and his breathing ragged. 'I can't do this. I **won't** do this.'

Then he was gone, yanking the door open and stumbling down the steps as though the very hounds of hell were after him. And as he ran, his eyes filled with tears and his heart filled with pain, and he cursed himself for being a fool for a second time.

Nelly watched him go. That was the second time he'd fled from her in as many weeks. But this time her heart was splintering into a thousand little pieces.

What an idiot she'd been. She'd practically thrown herself at him.

For the briefest of moments she'd thought he was as willing as she, that he'd wanted it as much as she had, but then he'd abruptly come to his senses. Then he'd made it clear that he didn't want her at all.

She didn't blame him for going along with it – shared history and all that. But as soon as his head had gained control of his body, he'd rejected her.

Swallowing convulsively, she sat down, balancing on the edge of one of the benches, and she forced herself not to cry.

'Nelly, are you okay? Did he…? Do you want me to…?' One of the brickies, Alan, was staring at her. 'I'll fetch Gavin, he'll know what to do.'

'Don't!' she barked, and Alan's eyebrows shot up, alarm on his face. Lowering her voice and softening her tone, she said, 'There's no need. Nothing happened. We were just catching up.'

Alan's gaze came to rest on her swollen mouth, then rose to her eyes. 'Right.'

She could sense his doubt, and she could also see the slight twitch of his lips. It didn't take a genius to work out what had been going on, and she stifled a groan. Everyone would know about it by knocking off time – before then, probably.

Despite her regret, she couldn't help thinking how good it had been to be held by Isaac. How it had felt like she was coming home, that in his arms were where she belonged. His kiss had been so sweet, so familiar, so damned **good**. She hadn't felt passion or desire like that since the last time he had made love to her, and her reaction to him shocked her to the bone.

Dimly she heard Alan leave, no doubt to spread the rumour that he'd caught the boss getting jiggy with the architect, but she didn't care.

All she could think about was Isaac. All the love she felt for him had come flooding back, engulfing her like a tidal wave, threatening to drown her. She'd never felt a fraction of what she felt for Isaac for any other man, and she knew now that she never would. She was a one-man woman, and unfortunately for her that man was Isaac: a man who had loved her once, but didn't love her any more.

How could she move on when she would never have anything as good to move on to?

With a cry of despair, she buried her head in her hands and tried not to weep. There would be plenty of time for crying in the lonely years ahead. But as she battled to keep her tears in check, she mourned his loss, and the loss of what they might have had together, of the love they might have shared, the memories they might have made, the babies they might have given life to.

And with that, Nelly gave in to her misery and cried for all the things that had been and all the things that weren't to be, and for the endless, loveless life ahead without the only man she would ever love.

Petra was in the feed room as she straightened up to watch Nelly trudge across the yard to the car park. The woman looked as though she had the weight of the world on her shoulders. Less than half an hour ago, Petra had spied Isaac doing the exact same thing, and she wondered if something was wrong.

She didn't think it was anything to do
with the build, because one or the other
of them would have told her. So if it
wasn't a work problem, she wondered if it
was anything to do with the sparks that
she'd noticed flying between them during
the meeting in the dining room a few
weeks ago.

She placed her hands in the small of her
back and rubbed absently, wincing.
Although she loved the concept of having
a baby, Petra wasn't too keen on the
reality of being pregnant.

Everything south of her neck was either
sore or ached. Starting with her boobs,
which had swollen to twice their normal
size and hurt if she so much as sneezed.
She'd found herself holding on to them
when she came down the stairs the other
day because the movement had caused

them to bounce painfully. Then there was her back, which for the past few weeks had ached like hell, and had ached more these past few days, if that was at all possible. Then there was her stomach, which looked as though she was carrying a whole litter of small humans inside it, and not just the one. There had only been a single baby on the scans, hadn't there? Surely two different sonographers couldn't have got that wrong, no matter how many babies she feared might be in there.

Besides being the size of a small moon, her tummy was as tight as a drum, and if she had any more Braxton Hicks, Petra thought she might scream. They flippin' hurt and were getting worse. She could have sworn they weren't as painful or as frequent this morning.

Then there was her waterworks. She didn't believe it was possible to need to go to the loo as often as she did. Three times a night was getting to be the norm. Maybe she'd be more accepting of her need to wee, if her ankles weren't so swollen. Kankles, that's what she had: she was clearly hanging onto more fluid than she was getting rid of. And her fingers had also expanded, forcing her to take her engagement ring off. She didn't want to think about what state she was going to be in by the time this baby arrived!

Petra had come to the conclusion that she was a mess, and the sooner this baby was born the better, as far as she was concer—

'What the hell?!' A kind of popping sensation came from down below, a sudden gush of wee behind it, followed by one of the worst Braxton Hicks contractions she'd experienced so far.

Contractions...?

Wee...? **That wasn't urine**.

Oh, no. No, no, no. This can't be happening. It was too soon, too early. The baby wasn't due for another five weeks.

Petra clutched her stomach, her hand cradling its weight. Reaching out to hold onto the wall for support, she staggered a couple of steps, then a couple more. She had to get to the house and find Amos to take her to the hospital. But first she had to phone Harry.

She couldn't cope with this without him.

CHAPTER SEVEN

Harry ran his hand down the hind leg of the horse he was about to shoe and lifted its hoof. The animal shifted its weight to compensate for having to stand on three feet, and flicked him in the face with its tail.

He'd shod this horse in the past, and another one belonging to the same owner. The gelding was a gentle old thing, well used to the procedure, and as Harry checked his hoof, he felt a soft nose nuzzling at one of his back pockets.

'Not yet, boy,' he chided. 'You know how this works – you get your treat **after** you've got new shoes on, not before.'

Harry let go of the hoof and, one hand on the horse's rump to let him know he was still there, he moved around the back of him to the other side.

He was just about to lift the other hind foot when his phone rang. 'Excuse me a sec,' he said to the horse's owner, and pulled his mobile out of the pocket the horse had been nosing at.

'Amos, what do you need me to get?' It wasn't unheard of for Amos to ask him to pick up a loaf of bread, or a four-pinter of milk, or something he'd forgotten which was needed for their dinner.

'Harry...?' Amos sounded odd, and a prickle of concern nibbled at the edge of Harry's mind.

'What is it, what's wrong?'

'It's Petra, she's gone into labour.'

'What do you mean? She can't have. It's too soon. It'll be those practice contractions – the Braxton Hicks things.'

'Her waters have broken and she's having proper contractions. Harry, Petra is definitely in labour.'

Oh, god! This couldn't be happening. The baby wasn't due for another five weeks.

'I'll be there in half an hour.' Harry had already started walking. He caught the horse owner's eye and shook his head. 'Sorry, I've... my fiancée, the baby,' he blurted, then he was running to his van, his heart beating madly, his stomach churning.

He heard Amos yelling down the phone as he ran. 'Harry! Don't come to the stables. Are you still there? I said, don't come to the stables. I'm taking her to the hospital.'

'Call an ambulance,' Harry instructed.

'I've spoken to her midwife – she's told me to take her to the maternity wing myself. No need for an ambulance. And, Harry?'

'What?' He yanked the van door open and threw himself inside.

'There's no need to drive like a maniac. They said it'll be ages yet before the baby's born.'

'He's going to be all right, isn't he?' Harry had never felt fear like this.

'He'll be fine,' Amos said. 'They both will.'

Harry believed him – to think otherwise would surely tear him apart.

Harry didn't remember a thing about his mad dash to the hospital. Despite Amos telling him there was no hurry, Harry couldn't help but get there as fast as he could, and he almost took the sharp corner into the hospital's main car park on two wheels, earning himself a glare from a driver on the opposite side of the road.

It took him ages to find a parking space, and at one point he seriously considered abandoning the van in front of a row of parked cars.

He was about to do just that, when he saw a car inch out of the space it was in. Another vehicle indicated its intention to park there, but Harry ignored it and he shot into the space, narrowly missing the waiting car.

'What the hell do you think you're playing at?' the irate driver yelled at him as Harry leapt out. 'Oi! Come back, that's my parking space!'

Harry ignored him, and sprinted across the car park at full pelt, almost falling in through the door leading to the maternity suite.

'Can I help you?' A receptionist sat behind a desk, and he skidded to a halt.

'Petra Kelly. In labour. Just brought in,' he panted. 'I'm the father. The baby's father. Not **her** father.'

The woman, clearly used to panicking expectant dads, smiled politely and checked the computer screen, as Harry bent forward, put his hands on his knees and panted.

'Ah, yes. She's in room 7. Down this corridor, turn left, then right.'

Harry was on his way before she'd finished speaking, calling a thank you over his shoulder. Now that he'd arrived, his heart rate slowed a little, but he still felt jittery from the adrenalin and his stomach continued to churn.

Sick and anxious, he paused for a moment to compose himself. The last thing Petra needed was for him to burst into the room in the state he was in. She'd be worried enough already, without him adding to it. He wanted to appear calm and steady, even though his emotions were all over the place.

Slowly, the smells and sounds of the hospital's maternity wing seeped under the panic he was feeling and brought him up short. Like all hospitals, the smell of antiseptic was paramount, but unlike any other hospital visits he'd made in the past, the noises emanating from various rooms made his hair stand on end. If he didn't know better, he'd think people were being tortured inside them.

Until now, he hadn't given much thought to the stark reality of the birthing process, but these women sounded as though they were in agony, and he shuddered at the realisation that Petra would be going through the same thing.

Suddenly it seemed very real.

He was about to become a father. **Today.** Him, Harry Milton, would be someone's dad before the day was out.

Tentatively, he knocked on the half-ajar door of room 7, and with a considerable degree of wariness, he stuck his head around the door.

As soon as Amos saw him, he heaved himself to his feet and ushered him back into the corridor. 'Thank god you're here,' Amos said croakily. 'They reckon she'll have it in the next few minutes. You'd better go in. I'll stay out here.' Amos was pale and his hands were shaking.

'Is she okay?' His heart was in his mouth as he waited for Amos's answer.

'In pain, as you'd expect, and scared. I think she just wants to get it over with and get the baby out. Go.' Amos pushed him towards the door. 'It's you she wants, not me.'

A guttural moan came from inside the labour suite, and Harry's eyes widened.

'Harreeeey!' Petra yelled. 'Get in here!! Ohhhh, bugger! It hurts!'

Harry took a deep breath and dived through the door.

He only had time for the words, 'Baby's head is crowning' to register, before someone grabbed his arm and propelled him to Petra's side. Three people were gathered at the business end and two more hovered around the room, and Harry had no idea what was going on and was too frightened to ask.

Petra had a sheet draped over her swollen stomach, and her hands were gripping the sides of the bed she was lying on. Her face was a screwed-up mask of effort and determination.

'The head is out. Stop pushing,' one of the gowned midwives instructed, and Petra slumped back, her cheeks red, her eyes brimming with unshed tears. She reached for Harry's hand and clutched it, and he winced as the small bones were crushed together, feeling helpless.

Bending to kiss her on the forehead, he stroked a strand of hair away from her damp face.

'It's okay, everything is okay,' he murmured, praying it was true. She was in the best place and in capable hands, as was the little scrap who was fighting to be born.

'Wait, wait...' the midwife urged as she knelt between Petra's legs. Petra let out a whimper of pain. 'Okay, when you feel your next contraction building, I want you to take a deep breath, then push as hard as you can for as long as you can.'

'It's coming,' Petra panted, and she inhaled sharply, then curled her chin into her chest and pushed.

Harry wasn't quite sure what happened next, but there was a flurry of activity, a scream of triumph from Petra, and suddenly there was a baby. A real baby. **His** baby.

Tears streaming down his face, he gulped back a sob.

The squirming, wriggling infant let out a choked gurgle, followed by an outraged cry, then he was quickly wrapped in a blanket and handed to a waiting nurse.

'We're just going to check him over, then you can hold him,' one of the midwives said. 'As I explained to Petra, Baby is a little early, so we want to make doubly sure he's okay.'

'Give him to me,' Petra demanded.

'In a minute, love. They're just going to check him over,' Harry told her.

'He's all right, isn't he?' She turned her worried gaze up at him.

'Apgar score six,' he heard someone say.

'What's that? Is it serious?' Panic flared in his chest.

A midwife was busy cleaning Petra up and Harry looked away, his attention on his son. She said, 'An Apgar test is given to all newborns immediately after birth to check heart rate, muscle tone, and so on. The score tells us whether Baby might need some additional help. Six suggests he may need a tiny bit of help.' She glanced up. 'Don't worry.'

Easier said than done, Harry thought.

He watched anxiously as his son was checked, weighed, then wrapped in a blanket, and he didn't take his eyes off the baby until he was placed in Petra's waiting arms.

Suddenly the tension drained out of him as Petra unwrapped the little boy to examine him.

The baby was perfect. Ten tiny fingers, ten tiny toes, a button nose, two little ears, a mop of hair plastered to his little head, and the most disgruntled expression Harry had ever seen on another human being.

One of the nurses said, 'Dad, would you like to hold him? Then we're going to take him to the Special Care Baby Unit.'

'Why?' Petra wailed, holding the baby closer. She looked as panicked as Harry felt.

'It's just a precaution,' the midwife soothed. 'Baby is five weeks and two days early, and he's a little on the small side, so he'll be kept in for a few days for monitoring.'

Desperate to hold his son but not wanting to take him away from Petra, Harry knelt by her side and wrapped his arms around the two of them. And as he did so, an overwhelming feeling of love swept through him. Their baby would be okay – he knew it. He **had** to be, because anything else was simply unthinkable.

Isaac didn't think Nelly could hurt him again, but she had, and this time it wasn't her fault. He could have left when he'd seen her van in the stables' car park. He could have refused her offer of tea. He could have walked out of the caravan when she'd started talking about the past. He could have let her leave, instead of grabbing her arm.

Could have, should have, would have... He was a grown man, responsible for his own actions and his own mistakes. And this mistake had been a biggie.

Isaac had gone from having an aching heart, to having it shattered again in the space of a few moments, and now he had to live with the consequences.

Maybe if she hadn't kissed him back with such ardour—?

Bah, don't go blaming her, he told himself. He should be adult enough to accept that the fault was his. Whether she was in a relationship with William or not, or whether she was merely hoping she could be, was neither here nor there. **Isaac** had kissed **her**, not the other way around. She'd not given him the slightest encouragement, so this current heartbreak was all his own fault this time.

He'd known he was playing with fire, but he'd stuck his hand in the flames and had got burnt.

Unable to face going back to the office, he detoured to his mum's house in the hope that she'd be in. He wouldn't burden her with his misery, but he just needed to be with someone who loved him, someone who was on his side and would fight his corner (if only she knew that a fight was needed). It would be a fight indeed to keep a hold on his despair and not let it show.

He was about to tell himself that his heart had healed once before and it could do so again, but he was forced to admit that it hadn't, had it? It hadn't healed at all – he'd just slapped a ruddy great big bandage on it to hold its shattered pieces together and had pretended everything was all right. It had taken seeing Nelly again to understand that he'd never got over her. And it had taken one kiss to understand that he never would.

'Hiya, love, I didn't expect you to call in today,' his mum said, when she saw him. She narrowed her eyes and tilted her head to the side. 'Is something wrong?'

'Not at all. I can pop in to see my mum if I want, can't I?' He gave her a customary kiss on the cheek.

She was looking brighter than the last time he'd seen her, less sorrowful somehow. But he'd seen her like this before, and he realised her grief over his dad leaving wasn't a constant thing – some days it was worse than others and she found it harder to cope. Today appeared to be one of her better days.

Isaac wished he knew why his parents' marriage had fallen apart. It wouldn't make any difference to the situation as such, but he wanted to understand. He could certainly empathise with his mum, because he felt Nelly's loss as keenly now as he had done back then. More so, after what had happened earlier. He wanted to tell his mum that things would get better, that she'd get over it eventually and move on. But it hadn't got any better for **him**, had it, and he didn't want to lie to her.

'Isaac!' Julie's voice was sharp.

'What?'

'You were miles away. Now, I know you say you're fine, but I'm your mother. You can't fool me: I can tell when you're upset. What's wrong? And don't say 'nothing', because I won't believe you.'

He hesitated. His mum had enough to be going on with, without adding his burden to the pile. She'd only worry, and he'd come back home to help her, not to cause her any more distress.

'You may as well tell me,' she insisted. 'If you don't, I'll only worry.

Once again, he cursed his impulsiveness. He should have gone back to work, not indulged in his need for comfort.

She sensed there was something wrong, so he may as well tell her, because she'd only keep on if he didn't, or think the worst. But where to start?

'Are you ill?' she demanded, concern creasing her brow.

'What? No! I'm as healthy as a horse.'

'Have you got money worries?'

'No more than anyone else.'

'The business is doing okay?'

'It's fine, Mum, honest.'

'That leaves one thing – a woman.'

His expression must have given him away because Julie cried. 'I'm right, aren't I? Tell me about it, Isaac. I might be able to help.'

'I doubt that very much.' He saw her face and sighed. 'Her name is Nelly and I met her in university, although she's originally from Picklewick and she still lives there.' He and Nelly had often marvelled that they only lived nine miles apart, yet it had taken a course in architecture in a university thirty-five miles away, to bring them together. Right now, Isaac wished he'd studied somewhere, **anywhere,** else.

'Picklewick. I see. Did you know her well?'

'I was in love with her.'

His mum blinked. 'Was she in love with you?'

'I thought so at the time, but I changed my mind when she dumped me and dropped out of the course.'

His mum nodded, and he saw understanding flit across her face. 'Your dad and I guessed something had happened, and we wondered whether it might be to do with a girl. But you didn't say anything and we didn't like to pry. It was in the middle of your second year, wasn't it? You seemed pretty upset.'

'I was.'

'This barn conversion that you're doing in Picklewick? Is it for her?'

'No, but I have bumped into her again.' He inhaled slowly, then let the breath out in a long sigh. 'The firm she owns is doing the renovations on the barn. It was because of that firm that she left uni. Her dad owned it and he became ill. Seriously ill, as it turned out. She left the course to run the company, but not before she ended our relationship. It broke my heart.'

'Oh, Isaac, I'm so sorry.' His mum's eyes filled with tears. 'First love can be so hard to get over.'

He put his arm around her and gave her a hug. 'I'm sorry, I shouldn't have said anything. I don't want to upset you.' At times like this Isaac wanted to take a swing at his father.

'I want you to feel you can share things with me. And I'm glad you told me. How do you feel about seeing her again?'

'I still love her.'

'Is that why you've never settled down? Your dad and I assumed it was because you hadn't found the right woman, or because you're only thirty-two and you didn't want to settle down yet.'

'The problem is that I **did** find the right woman, but she didn't want me,' he admitted, fresh pain coursing through him.

'Do you think she used the fact that her dad was ill as an excuse to end your relationship?'

'Good lord, no!'

'Then why did she?'

'I assumed it was because she never really loved me in the first place.'

'Have you looked at it from her point of view?'

'Not then. I was too young and too wrapped up in my own misery to look at it sensibly. I didn't appreciate how ill her father was, nor the extent of her sense of duty.'

'But you do now? Duty is why you moved from Wiltshire,' she reminded him.

'You needed me, Mum. After what Dad did—'

His mum closed her eyes slowly, and when she opened them again, he saw they were filled with anguish. 'Your father didn't do anything. It was me – I'm the one to blame.'

'For what?' Isaac was puzzled.

'For your dad and I splitting up.'

'Why? I don't understand.'

'I had an affair,' his mum said starkly.

'Pardon?' Isaac couldn't imagine his staid, sensible mother having an affair. He must have misheard.

'It's true,' she assured him. 'This isn't your dad's fault.'

'Who did you have an affair with? Why?'

'You don't know him. It was before you were born. He was the love of my life, but I was married to your father and no matter how much it hurt, I put duty to your dad before love. Don't get me wrong, I loved your father deeply – I still do. But I loved Emrys more.'

'But if this happened before I was born...?'

'He died last year, and when I found out I fell apart. Your dad quite rightly didn't understand why I was in such a state, so I had to tell him.'

'**That's** why he left?'

His mum nodded. 'It might have been a long time ago, but I betrayed your dad, and he can't forgive me. I don't blame your father. I haven't forgiven myself, either. The reason I'm telling you this is twofold. The first is that I don't want you to go blaming your dad or jumping to conclusions – I know you were thinking that he might have been unfaithful.'

Isaac shrugged. It had crossed his mind. 'And the other reason?'

'If you still love Nelly, you should tell her. I know how it feels to think you have to do the right and moral thing, and I suspect so does she. I also suspect she was setting you free because she loved you too much to tie you down. You see, I couldn't commit to Emrys in the end, so I ended the affair. I did it out of love for him.'

'And you regret it now?' He pulled a face. 'I'm kind of glad you did, or I wouldn't be here.'

'That's where you're wrong. I ended it when I found out I was pregnant.'

'What!?'

'Take that look off your face, Isaac – Emrys isn't your father. But I couldn't deny your dad the chance to be a full-time father to you. If I'd left him for Emrys, he would hardly have seen you. You see, Emrys was about to emigrate to New Zealand, and he wanted me to go with him. As much as I wanted to, and as much as it broke my heart to end it with him, I couldn't do that to your dad. I told Emrys it was over and that it had been just a fling. I told him it was your father who I truly loved, and I sent him away.'

'Oh, Mum.'

'I had to, because if Emrys had had any idea of my true feelings he would never have emigrated. So I set him free. I don't know Nelly and I don't know her side of the story, just the part you've shared with me, but from what you've told me, I think she might have been setting you free, too. Not because she didn't love you enough, but because she loved you too much.'

Isaac was lost for words. He was stunned and in a state of disbelief. Who knew his mother had such hidden depths? He'd taken his parents' love for each other at face value and had never thought to question it.

'Is there any chance of you and Dad getting back together?' he asked.

'Probably not. There's been too much water under the bridge, too much has happened, so much bitterness, so much heartache. It might be too late for me and your dad, but it might not be too late for you and Nelly. If you still care for her, then you've got to find out if she cares for you, too.'

At night the ward was quiet. The occasional soft squeak of a nurse's shoe, the murmur of a new mother and the occasional cry of a tiny baby were the backdrop to Petra's wakefulness.

She was in a side room off the main ward, which she was grateful for. The thought of seeing mothers with their new babies when hers was in the special care unit would have been difficult. Just thinking about him made her heart constrict with longing and her arms ache to hold him. She felt empty and bereft, and tears were perilously close to the surface. Petra didn't cry often, but since the surprise arrival of her baby earlier today, that was all she seemed to have done.

Sore, shocked, scared, vulnerable… Petra had never felt so weepy in her life, and she wished Harry was by her side to give her strength.

Even as a tear or two trickled down her cheek, she knew she should be grateful.

Her baby was healthy, and throughout her pregnancy that was all she'd prayed for.

'All right, my love?' A nurse popped her head around the door.

'Fine,' Petra whispered back, then a sob escaped her, giving lie to what she'd just said.

The nurse slipped inside and automatically reached for Petra's wrist, checking her pulse. 'Do you want me to take you to the special care unit?'

'Now?' Petra's heart leapt.

'Yes. You can see your baby whenever you want. There's no restriction on mums visiting their babies. The only thing I'd say is that you make sure you get enough rest. Spend some time with your baby, then come back to bed and try to sleep.'

She smiled gently at her. 'You'll soon wish you'd taken my advice when you get him home.'

Petra nodded, but she knew she wouldn't be able to sleep. She was too emotional, too strung out, and worry had settled in her chest like a stone. She'd been told that her baby was doing well, that him being in the unit was merely a precaution, and that she'd probably be able to take him home in the next few days, but it didn't stop her fretting.

'Have you decided on a name?' the nurse asked her, as they travelled down in the lift. Amos, bless him, had waited until he knew that she and the baby were okay, then as soon as he knew she was being kept in overnight, he'd dashed back to the stables to fetch her some pyjamas, a dressing gown and a pair of slippers.

Petra secured that dressing gown more firmly around her middle, and thought for a moment.

She and Harry had batted a few ideas around, but nothing had seemed quite right, so they'd decided to wait until the baby was born, in the hope that something would leap out at them. They had considered naming him Gregory, after Harry's father, but although Harry had been touched by Petra's suggestion, he'd pointed out that her dad might feel a bit put out.

Petra hadn't given a hoot. They might be her parents, but she wasn't as close to them as she might have been. Since she'd come to live at the stables, she'd only seen them once or twice a year, and phone calls were also infrequent. Amos had played a much larger part in her life since she turned eighteen so, if anything, she'd prefer to name the baby after him instead. Now, that was an idea...

Gregory Amos Milton, Amos Gregory Milton: both combinations sounded good, but Petra felt that neither of them were quite right.

'Here we are,' the nurse said as the lift came to a halt and the doors pinged open. 'Do you remember the way from here?'

Petra did. She and Harry had been shown to the unit not long after their son had been taken there, and she'd never forget the sight of him, wrapped up like a burrito, his little face scrunched and red, as he lay in a plastic cot.

As she approached, she saw his delicate blue-veined eyelids fluttering as he slept.

What was he dreaming about, she wondered. What dreams did a newborn have? She wished she knew, and she wished Harry was here by her side so she could share her thoughts with him.

Her baby's cheek was softer than a cherry blossom petal, and she stroked his skin, her heart so full with love for this tiny human that she thought it might burst. He was perfect, and he looked so peaceful that she simply knew everything was going to be okay.

Petra smiled with sudden joy: she **knew** her baby's name and it was a wonderful blend of the names of the two men who had shaped her and Harry.

Amory.

CHAPTER EIGHT

'What time is it?' Harry asked

Amos glanced at him as he stumbled, haunted-eyed and tousled-haired, into the kitchen, and said, 'Five-thirty.' He flipped the switch on the kettle. Amos had been up for at least an hour, so he could do with another cup of tea.

'Oh, god.' Harry sank into a chair, put his elbows on the table and rested his head in his hands. 'I think I managed to sleep for about three-quarters of an hour. How about you?'

Amos had been dog-tired after he'd returned from the hospital, his emotions all over the place, but he'd not been able to sleep until he heard Harry come in some time after eleven, and even then his sleep had been fitful and restless. Yesterday had taken a toll on everyone, Petra most of all.

'So, so,' he replied. He had a feeling his sleep would be interrupted for a few months to come. He'd heard that babies liked to wake in the middle of the night, and they didn't care who else they disturbed in the process. He didn't mind, though – the thought of having a baby in the house was exciting. He just wished Mags was alive to see it – she would have doted on the little mite. So much so, that Petra probably wouldn't have got a look in. It was one of the major regrets in his life, that he and Mags hadn't been blessed with children. God knows they'd tried, but it wasn't meant to be.

He was intensely grateful for the opportunity to be a grandfather. As far as he was concerned Petra was his daughter, so any children of hers would be his grandkids. She was actually his great-niece, but whatever the physical relationship, the emotional one was the one that mattered.

'Petra thinks she'll be coming home this morning,' Harry said, taking his head out of his hands and curling his fingers around the steaming mug that Amos placed on the table in front of him.

'You've spoken to her already?'

'We've been messaging back and forth all night, off and on. I don't think she's slept much either.'

Amos hesitated to ask the next question. 'Will...erm...the baby be coming home today, too?'

Harry pulled a face, his eyes hooded. 'I don't think so. I'd be surprised if he did.' He brightened. 'You haven't seen him yet – shall I ask if you can visit?'

Harry had shown him a photo when Amos had dashed back to the hospital with stuff for Petra, but Amos longed to see the child in the flesh. 'That would be wonderful. I'm desperate to give the little fella cuddle. Has Petra told her parents yet? Or do you want me to do it?'

Petra wasn't as close to her parents as she could have been, and it didn't help that they lived so far away. Norwich – which was where Faith, Charity's twin, now also lived – wasn't exactly at the other end of the earth, but Petra never seemed to find the time to make the journey, and she'd only seen them once in the past year, when she'd introduced them to Harry. It was sad, but Amos got the impression that Harry and Petra's dad hadn't hit it off. And Petra wanting Amos to give her away, and not her own father, spoke volumes, in Amos's opinion.

'I don't think she has told them,' Harry said, breaking into Amos's thoughts. 'What with everything that happened yesterday...'

'She'd better call them. They'll want to see her, and the baby.'

Harry rubbed a hand over his face. 'I'll remind her, if she hasn't already done it. I'll give it a couple of hours, then go to the hospital. Is there anything you need me to do here before I go?'

'Nothing. Nathan and October will have it covered. I've told both of them what's going on. Just concentrate on Petra and the baby. And tell Petra not to worry: I know what she's like when it comes to the stables. We can manage perfectly well without her.'

'Make sure you don't do too much,' Harry warned. 'The last thing we need is for you to be ill.'

Amos wrinkled his nose. His angina was a source of ongoing irritation, but he just had to put up with it. He knew his limitations, and there was no way he was going to add to Petra and Harry's burden by doing something that might bring on an attack.

Harry told him that he and Petra would probably spend the day at the hospital, so after Harry left (with a change of clothes for Petra and strict instructions from Amos that they had to eat a proper meal at lunchtime) Amos updated the list of things that needed to be done today on the whiteboard, and left a note to ask if October could take the jumping class that was scheduled for later. He didn't want to cancel classes unless he had to, because every pound was vital. Despite Harry investing a significant amount in the holiday cottages project, Amos was determined not to let him pay for all of it, so it was imperative that any scheduled classes or hacks went ahead.

He'd just finished writing the last item on the whiteboard and was turning his mind to what needed doing inside the house when October appeared, and she wasn't alone. Lena was with him.

'Hello,' he said in surprise. 'What are you doing here? Has October persuaded you to take up riding?'

'I'll have you know, I used to ride quite a lot when I was younger. And so did my mum. She taught October to ride.'

'Well, I never! I hadn't realised Olive used to ride.' Amos squinted at Lena, as an idea occurred to him. 'Do you think she'd like to pay a visit to the stables?'

'I'm sure she'd love to. That's very kind of you. But not for a bit, eh? You'll have enough to be going on with for a while. How is Petra and the baby?'

'Harry thinks she'll be home later today, but the baby won't be allowed home for a few more days. Anyway, what can I do for you?'

'I think it's more a case of what **I** can do for **you**. October was telling me that Petra and Harry haven't set up the nursery yet.'

'No, they haven't,' Amos confirmed, wondering where the conversation was heading.

'Shall we get started?' Lena rolled up her sleeves. 'There's lots to do to get ready for the little one's arrival, and I suspect the proud parents won't be spending a great deal of time at the stables while the baby is in hospital. Have they decided on a name for him?'

'Er, no, not as far as I know.' Bemused Amos wondered what it was that she wanted to get started on.

'Show me which room is going to be the nursery, and I'll fetch the cleaning stuff from the car.'

'We've got cleaning stuff here,' he protested. 'And I can do that myself.'

'I like using what I like using,' Lena stated firmly. 'Now, don't argue. You're going to need all the help you can get. And once you've shown me where to go, you can put the kettle on. Oh, and we've had a whip round in the village and I've brought a load of stuff that Petra and Harry might need for the baby. If she already has some of it, I can take what she doesn't want to the charity shop. It won't go to waste. There are some of the dinkiest clothes you've ever seen, perfect for premature babies. How much did he weigh?'

Amos stood there with his mouth open, his eyes wide, and his heart full. If he'd been awed by people's generosity when they'd come to help clear the cow shed, he was positively overcome with gratitude now. He felt tears gathering behind his eyes and when he tried to stutter out his thanks, his voice was croaky with emotion.

'Chop, chop!' Lena said. 'That cot isn't going to put itself together. And the more we get done today, the less we'll have to do tomorrow. Before you know it, that little baby will be home and then your troubles will start.'

Amos smiled widely. Despite her no-nonsense attitude, Lena's voice was filled with warmth and positivity, and Amos knew she was right. His life, and the life of everyone at the stables would never be the same again, and he relished the thought.

Isaac rose earlier than usual, having hardly slept a wink all night. He hadn't been able to stop thinking about what his mum had told him.

That she'd managed to keep it a secret for so many years shocked him, until he remembered that he'd kept his love for Nelly under wraps and he'd also managed to hide his broken heart.

It had taken finding out that the love of her life was dead, for his mum's secret to come out. Her grief had been too profound to conceal from his father, Isaac realised. Then he wondered whether his own heartbreak had led to him moving so far away from his hometown. He was aware that the risk of running into Nelly had played a part, but had he also had a subconscious urge to hide his pain from his parents? He'd tried to bury it so deep that he'd convinced himself that he was over her, that she was his past.

It had taken meeting her again to understand that neither thing was true. He was as in love with her now as he had been then, and she would never be his past, not when he carried her with him constantly.

He could fully appreciate the pain his mum felt and was still feeling, but he also wished his mum and dad would try to work through this. They'd been happy before and maybe they could be happy again. Isaac had never once had the feeling that his parents didn't love each other. In fact, as far as he'd been able to tell, even with the benefit of hindsight he still thought the love they'd had for each other had been immense, and love like that didn't simply disappear like dawn mist on a summer morning. It was still there, somewhere, if only he could tap into it and remind them of it.

It might be too late for him and Nelly, but it wasn't too late for his parents. So, with that in mind, he set off to his father's house. It was about time the two of them had a proper talk.

'I know what happened between you and Mum,' was the first thing he said when his dad answered the door.

Stephen stared at him in silence for a heartbeat or two, then nodded slowly. 'I see. You'd better come in. Tea? Coffee? I haven't had my morning cuppa, yet.'

'Coffee, please. Have you got time to talk?'

'I've always got time for my son. Work can wait.' His dad was a teacher, and an inspiring one, at that. He hesitated, then said over his shoulder as he walked down the hall and into the kitchen, Isaac following, 'She told you about Emrys?' He sounded resigned, his voice flat. There wasn't a hint of emotion when he said Emrys's name.

'She did, but only because she was trying to put something into perspective, something about me, not you guys.'

'Oh?' His dad lifted two mugs off the mug tree and placed them on the countertop. He looked tired and worn. The months since the split hadn't been easy on him, and he was showing every one of his sixty-one years.

Isaac said abruptly, 'I thought you were going to retire when you got to sixty. Wasn't that the plan?'

'It was. Things change.'

Isaac heard the unspoken reason. Emrys had died and his mum had fallen apart. He wondered whether his dad had decided to keep working for financial reasons or for emotional ones. Looking at him, he guessed it might be the latter.

'What was she trying to put into perspective?' his dad asked.

Isaac swallowed. 'I met a girl when I was in university. She dropped out because her dad was ill.' He paused. 'I was in love with her. I still am.' Then he told his father all about her.

When he'd finished, his dad said, 'I knew Ken. It was a shame he was taken so young. From what I've heard, his daughter has done a brilliant job of keeping the business going.' His lips quirked. 'Your mum and I thought there was something up and we guessed it might be to do with a girl, but you didn't say anything and we didn't like to pry. You should have told us; a trouble shared is a trouble halved, so they say.'

'What was the point? She'd made her decision.'

'Like your mum said, we might have been able to put it into perspective.' Stephen gave him a dry look. 'You were too close.'

'Like you are, you mean?'

'Fair point. But your mum and I are married – that's the difference. She was unfaithful, and I'm not sure I can forgive that.'

'The hurt is the same. Dad, Nelly was The One, and I let her walk away. Mum is your One. Are you going to let something that happened nearly forty years ago wreck everything?'

'She still loves Emrys.'

'He's dead. You're not. And I believe she's grieving for you just as much as she's grieving for him.'

'Are you grieving too?'

Isaac dropped his head and nodded.

'How about you follow your own advice?' his dad suggested.

'It's too late. She's seeing the guy who manages the care home.'

'William Reid?' Stephen started to laugh.

'What's so funny?'

'William is gay.'

'He is?' Isaac blinked in astonishment. He could have sworn he'd seen a spark between them, or if not on William's part, then certainly on Nelly's. How wrong could he have been?

His dad nodded. 'Believe me, there's nothing going on between William and your girl.'

'She's not my girl.'

'She could be – if you asked her. Did she kiss you back?'

'Dad!'

'Did she?'

Isaac shrugged, feeling like a teenager who'd been caught snogging in the park. 'I suppose.'

'There you go, then. Look Isaac, you can either go for it – what have you got to lose? – or you can mope about and be forever wondering **what if.**'

'What about you and mum? I could say the same about you, because the pair of you are miserable without the other.'

'We'll see.' His dad sighed and his shoulders drooped, but not before Isaac saw a glimmer of hope in his father's eyes.

With a sigh, Isaac realised he had done as much as he could; the rest was up to his parents. What he needed to do now was to concentrate on his own happiness – and he strongly suspected that it was inextricably linked to a certain female builder.

Had she done the right thing in dropping out of university and ending her relationship with Isaac? It was a question Nelly had been asking herself, and it had kept her awake for the second night in a row. She was exhausted, physically and emotionally, and wished she could stop thinking about him, but Isaac invaded her thoughts as thoroughly as weeds invaded a garden if left unchecked. The problem was she couldn't control her thoughts: there was no equivalent of weed killer for the mind, and whatever she tried to occupy herself with, they kept returning to Isaac.

The kiss was the predominant thing dominating her thoughts, closely followed by the look on Isaac's face when he'd left: dismay, shock, and had she seen a hint of revulsion?

She wasn't sure, but whatever expression she thought she might have seen, one thing was abundantly clear – Isaac didn't want anything to do with her. The love he'd once felt had well and truly died, and her heart was breaking all over again.

Not that it had actually mended: for thirteen years it had been held together with sticking plaster and string.

She pottered around her kitchen, making herself a breakfast she wasn't able to face and psyching herself up to go to the stables, something else she couldn't face but knew she must. Gavin knew what he was doing and she had total faith in him, but she always, always performed daily checks on whatever jobs they had on. Sometimes it was just the one site, sometimes it was two, but she never failed to show her face, and if they were a man down or additional hands were needed, she'd get stuck in.

The only thing she wanted to get stuck into today was her duvet. The idea of going back to bed, pulling the covers over her head and sinking back into the oblivion of sleep was tempting, but if she put so much as one step on that slippery slope, she feared she might slide into a black hole of despair, never to emerge.

Had she been wrong to drop the course and drop Isaac?

'Stop it!' she cried, clapping her hands to her head. If she asked herself that question one more time she might scream. What was done, was done. There was no going back, no pressing rewind. Hindsight is a wonderful thing, because if she'd known back then that she would still be in love with him and that her heart would be just as broken thirteen years later, maybe she wouldn't have given up her dreams. But then again, how could she have done anything less and still be able to live with herself? She hadn't dropped everything on a whim – she'd done it for her **dad**.

Anyway, who was to say that their love would have stood the test of time? They may well have got to the end of their third year and have split up anyway. The relationship might have run its course and they would have gone their separate ways. Perhaps she was only feeling so bad simply because there was unfinished business between them, and no other reason.

That kiss hadn't felt like unfinished business, though.

'Stop thinking about it,' she commanded, then snorted. It was like trying to hold back the tide, and she was also starting to talk to herself. 'Nelly Newsome, you're falling apart.'

It took Nelly a second to realise that someone was ringing her doorbell, and with a sigh she threw her uneaten toast out of the window for the birds to feast on, and went to answer it.

Expecting it to be the postman (although if it was, he was early) she almost fainted when she saw Isaac standing on her step. Dizzily she put a hand on the frame to steady herself, and willed her racing heart to slow down.

God help her if she continued to react in this manner every time she clapped eyes on him.

'Can we talk?' he asked.

She tried to gauge his mood but failed. Was he here to apologise? To remonstrate with her? With her heart in her mouth, she stood to the side. 'You'd better come in.'

He stepped past and she caught his scent, her nostrils flaring as she inhaled. Her tummy turned over and she tottered after him on unsteady legs. Abruptly she wished she'd washed her hair and put some make-up on. She was keenly aware that she looked as bad as felt, and she didn't want him to think he was the cause.

'How do you know where I live?' she blurted, as he came to a halt at the end of the hall wondering whether he should go on into her lounge. She waved him inside. Is that the best you can do, she asked herself? There were much more important things going on here, and all she could think of was how he'd got hold of her address?

'Amos told me, but if he hadn't, I would have gone to your Mum's house. Although, she mightn't have taken kindly to a strange man turning up on her doorstep and asking for her daughter's address.' He turned to face her, and she saw that he didn't look much better than she did.

'She would have sent you away with a flea in your ear,' Nelly confirmed.

'I take it you never told her about me?'

'Not really, but even if I had, I doubt she would have remembered. She had other things going on at the time.' Nelly didn't see the point in telling him that her mum knew about him now.

'Of course she did.' He shuffled awkwardly from foot to foot. 'I'm sorry I kissed you.'

'Gee, thanks.' Her voice dripped with sarcasm and a flutter of annoyance replaced some of the pain she was feeling. It was better than the heartache, even though her ire wouldn't last.

'I didn't mean it like that. What I meant, was... Oh, hell, I don't know what I meant, except that I still love you.' He stopped, an anguished expression spreading across his face. He rubbed the back of his neck and swallowed convulsively.

Nelly was frozen. Even her churning thoughts had come to a halt. 'What?' she squeaked.

'Sorry, I shouldn't have come here. I knew it was a mistake, but my mum had Emrys and she didn't want me to be like her, and Dad...' He trailed off.

'What?' she asked again, confused. Has she heard him correctly? Or was she having some kind of an episode?

'Forget it. I'd better go.' He took a step towards the door, but Nelly was blocking his way and her feet refused to move.

She was frozen to the spot. 'Did you say—' she cleared her throat '—that you love me?'

'Forget it. I shouldn't have said anything. You clearly don't feel the same.'

'I do.'

'Erm... what?' His eyes bored into her.

'I love you, too.'

'You do?'

'Yes.' Her voice was stronger. This was crunch time – if she didn't tell him how she felt now, she never would. His declaration had taken her by surprise, but she realised he meant what he said. His love for her was written all over his face. It was a look she knew well, but one she didn't think she'd ever see again, and it made her soul sing.

His eyes softened. 'My mum explained why you ended things between us.'

'Your mum?' What did she know about this? Nelly had never met his mum.

'It's a long story, but we've got the rest of our lives for me to tell it.' His certainty took her breath away.

'We have?'

'If you want me.'

'Oh, I want you, all right,' she replied throatily, her tummy fizzing, her chest aching from sheer joy, and her heart threatening to leap out of her ribcage. 'I always have.'

'Thirteen years,' he began, then laughed quietly. 'It doesn't matter. I've found you again – that's what's important.'

He enfolded her in his arms, and his mouth came down on hers. Eagerly she kissed him back, melting into his embrace.

His fingers tangled in her hair, holding her close, and she had the feeling he didn't intend to let her go. Ever.

Finally though, she tore her lips away from his, feeling thoroughly kissed, her body and her mind in total disarray. She wanted to drag him off to bed and make love to him for the rest of the day, week, month, but she wasn't going to. As he'd pointed out, they had the rest of their lives together: she wanted to get to know him all over again, to thoroughly understand the man he'd become, to know him inside and out before she reacquainted herself with his body.

It was going to be fun, this exploration of hers, but she had a feeling she wouldn't hold out for long. She was as eager for him as he was for her, but a short wait would do them both good.

Anyway, she wanted to hear those three little words again. And again, and again...

CHAPTER NINE

'Now what?' Harry asked.

Petra wrinkled her nose. They were standing in their son's gorgeous nursery, staring down into his cot. They'd only brought him home this morning, and the little boy had been cuddled constantly since they'd lifted him out of his car seat.

It was now early evening. Amory had been fed, he'd been winded, he'd been topped and tailed, and he'd had a fresh nappy on. Then he'd been placed carefully in his brand new cot, with the soft white sheet and the colourful mobile hanging over it. A night light glowed in the corner and the soothing sounds of a human heartbeat emanated from an iPod on top of the brand new chest of drawers.

It was a perfect room for a baby.

Unfortunately, Amory didn't think so.

From the second his little bottom had touched the mattress, he'd howled. His cheeks had reddened, and he'd screwed up his face, opened his mouth, and bawled.

Petra had immediately scooped him back out again and cuddled him close. Amory had immediately stopped crying.

Reassured that nothing was seriously wrong, she'd checked his nappy again, Harry looking on anxiously, then she'd tried him with some milk, but the baby had only taken a few desultory sucks and had then fallen asleep with her nipple in his mouth.

So she and Harry had tried to put him down again.

Slowly, careful not to disturb Amory, she'd placed him back in his cot, and the pair of them had tiptoed out of the room, holding their breath.

They'd made it as far as the top of the stairs before their son let out a squawk of indignation, quickly followed by a full-throated bellow.

In resignation, she and Harry had returned to the nursery, to find Amory with a screwed-up face and angrily waving arms. His tiny hands were curled into fists and his legs kicked and jerked.

He clearly wasn't happy.

'What do you think is wrong with him?' Petra asked, anxiously.

'I don't know.' Harry was equally as worried.

'Shall I pick him up again?' she wondered.

'Better had. We can't let him cry like this.'

'Do you think we should phone the out-of-hours doctor?'

'If he doesn't stop crying...' Harry agreed.

Petra picked her baby up and held him against her chest. Amory stopped crying so abruptly it was as though a switch had been turned off.

Petra looked at Harry. Harry gazed solemnly back at her.

Wordlessly, she put the baby back in his cot.

The switch was immediately reactivated, and Amory began to cry once more.

'At least we know what's wrong with him,' Harry said, raising his voice so he could be heard over the sounds his furious son was making.

'What do we do?' she asked. 'Do we leave him to cry?'

'I don't think I can stand it,' Harry said. 'It breaks my heart seeing him so upset.' This time it was Harry who plucked the irate infant from his cot.

Once again the noise ceased, but Amory didn't drop back off to sleep straight away. Instead, he lay there in the crook of his father's arm and gazed up at him with mistrustful eyes.

'He's waiting for me to put him back down,' Harry said in wonderment. 'Look at his little face.'

Petra didn't need to be told. She'd hardly taken her gaze off her baby since he'd been born, and only then it had been because she'd had to leave the hospital to go home to sleep. Now that he was home, she hadn't been able to tear her gaze away from him.

She turned in a slow circle, scanning the nursery. It was a warm and tranquil place. Lena and Amos had worked wonders, and she would be eternally grateful for their help and for the generosity of everyone in Picklewick. But she had a feeling the room wasn't going to be used as much as she'd assumed it would be. Not unless she and Harry moved their double bed into it and they slept in there until he was ready to sleep on his own. Which might be a good few years away.

'I wish babies came with an instruction manual,' she groaned. 'A definitive one. Because all those baby books Lena brought give different advice. No two say the same thing.'

'What should we do?' Harry asked. He was still staring into his baby's eyes and the baby was staring back at him. 'He knows we're talking about him.'

'Of course he does. He's a bright little boy, aren't you, poppet? He's also got us wrapped around his little finger.'

'He's only been home five minutes, and he's already calling the shots,' Harry agreed. 'What's he going to be like in a month's time?'

'I've no idea.' Petra wound her arms around Harry's waist and rested her head on his shoulder. 'But I can't wait to find out.'

'Neither can I, my love, neither can I.'

'This is better than the student union,' Isaac said to Nelly. They were having their first proper date in thirteen years. Nelly had made him wait until Friday, although they'd seen each other every day since they'd declared their love. They were currently in the Black Horse, perusing the menu. Nelly had insisted he wined and dined her, but she hadn't been bothered about going anywhere posh, because tonight was the night she intended making love to him, and she didn't have much of an appetite.

'We had some fun though, didn't we?' he was saying. 'Remember when that girl with the green and pink hair came on to me? You were furious.' He chuckled.

'I had every right to be,' Nelly replied loftily. 'She soon scarpered when I told her to get lost.'

'Yeah, you were quite scary when you were cross.'

'It's because I've been giving as good as I get with chippies and brickies ever since I was small. I wonder what she's doing now?'

'She's got a husband, four kids and a hairdressing salon.'

'Really? Good for her. I don't think I can remember seeing her with the same hair colour or style twice.' Nelly sipped at her wine. 'Do you keep in touch with many of the people we knew?'

'A few. There's a Facebook group where some of the students in our year hang out.' He inclined his head to the side and regarded her thoughtfully. 'Would you ever consider going back to uni and finishing your degree?'

'I don't think so. My mum asked me the same thing, but I'm happy doing what I'm doing.' She giggled. 'We could always join forces – you plan it and I'll build it.'

'Isn't that what we're doing now at the stables on Muddypuddle Lane?' he asked, staring at her.

'I suppose it is. It's what my dad and I intended to do.' She was wistful for a moment, but only for a moment. This was the start of a whole new life. It was time she looked forward, not back – she'd done enough of that over the years. If it came about that she and Isaac joined forces workwise, it would be the icing on the cake.

But first of all, there was something else she wanted to do. How hungry are you?' she asked, catching her bottom lip with her teeth and looking at him from beneath her lashes.

The flare of desire in his eyes made her heart thump erratically. 'Oh, I'm starving,' he replied huskily, 'but I think you know it's not food I want. It's **you**.' And with that he stood up, grabbed her hand, and they raced outside.

They had thirteen years of catching up to
do…

Despite Amos being out in the yard, he
could hear the baby's furious crying, and
he chuckled to himself.

'Listen to that,' he said to Star. 'Be
thankful your little one doesn't make such
a racket.' If anyone was listening, it might
sound as though he was complaining, but
he wasn't. He was proud – the little boy
had a sterling set of lungs on him, and
despite only being home for less than a
day, he was already making his presence
felt.

The mare flicked her ears and continued
to munch on the hay net. Her foal
mouthed at it, but Amos knew it was
more out of curiosity than any desire to

eat the dried stalks, although that would soon come. He was happy enough to nibble at the sweet grass when he and his mum were in the small paddock behind the house, but he'd yet to discover the delights of fresh hay.

Amos clicked his tongue and held out his hand. Cautiously the colt stepped towards him, his neck stretched, his nostrils wide. Suppressing a laugh, Amos felt the foal's soft nose tickle his palm. The little horse was growing in confidence every day, and so was his mum. She was now happy to be handled and groomed, although everyone was still careful around her. Since she'd arrived at the stables, she'd been shown nothing but love, and Amos was confident that she would eventually settle enough to be ridden. Not yet, though; she had a foal at foot, and that was enough for her to be going on with.

One thing Amos was determined about, was that neither Star nor her foal would be leaving the stables on Muddypuddle Lane. He'd been in touch with Sandra from the horse charity and had offered them a permanent home. The mare would probably never be suitable for the riding school, but maybe Megan would like to take her under her wing?

And as for the little colt, who they'd called Breeze for no other reason than October had liked the name, Amos had plans for him. The animal would be Amory's horse, and he and the baby could grow up together.

Amos sighed contentedly, his heart full of love and gratitude. His family was growing, as was the stables, and he couldn't wait to hear the patter of tiny feet (and hooves) as Amory and the foal enjoyed a whole world of wonderful adventures.

Nelly's bedroom was dark and silent, apart from the muted gleam of a streetlight outside, and Isaac's soft breathing. She could tell he wasn't asleep, but she didn't feel the need to say anything. Their bodies and their passion had been words enough, and they were happy to simply lie together in the afterglow, cocooned in the certainty of their love for each other.

Content for the moment to lay her head on his chest and to have his strong arms holding her close, Nelly couldn't remember ever feeling as blissful as she did right now. This rediscovered love of theirs was deeper and more profound, a more mature version of the heat and excitement of those early years. This, she knew, was going to last. She felt the conviction deep in her heart and it brought her to soft tears.

Isaac must have sensed them, because he gently extricated his arm and propped himself up on his elbow, his face close to hers as he stared into her eyes, searching, worrying.

'I love you,' she said.

'Why are you crying?' Isaac touched a finger to the trickle of moisture.

'Because I'm happy. I didn't realise how unhappy I had been until now.'

'I love you, too,' he said. 'More than you will ever know.' He took a breath and let it out slowly. She felt the warmth of it on her cheek. 'I don't know how I lived without you,' he whispered. 'Promise you won't leave me again.'

'I promise. I can't.' Another tear escaped. 'You are part of me – how could I leave?'

Isaac continued to look into her eyes and Nelly felt as though she was drowning in the love she saw in them.

No, not drowning – she was floating, buoyed up by his adoration and his naked longing and hunger for her. He was her "The One", and she was his, and now that she'd found him again, Nelly Newsome had no intention of ever letting him go.

The Stables on Muddypuddle Lane Series

Spring

Summer

Autumn

Winter

Valentine Kisses

The Patter of Tiny Feet

Wedding Bells

Christmas

About Etti

Etti Summers is the author of wonderfully romantic fiction with happy ever afters guaranteed.

She is also a wife, a mum, a pink gin enthusiast, a veggie grower and a keen reader.

www.ingramcontent.com/pod-product-compliance
Lightning Source LLC
Chambersburg PA
CBHW050809190726
48285CB00005B/1849